WHAT I NEVER TOLD YOU

WHAT I NEVER TOLD YOU

Stories

. . .

Rebecca Lawton

WAVEGIRL BOOKS

AGUA CALIENTE • SONOMA

The author and publisher make grateful acknowledgment to the following individuals and organizations for giving their permission to reprint excerpts from copyrighted works:

Earlier versions of all stories in *What I Never Told You: Stories*, © 2014 Rebecca Lawton. All rights reverted from Little Curlew Press, LLC, Sarasota, Florida. Used by permission.

Wavegirl Books: beccalawton.com

International Standard Book Number: 978-0-9777856-5-0
E-book ISBN: 978-0-9777856-6-7
Library of Congress Control Number: 2022921584
Second Edition 2022

Cover photo: "Soft Rocks, Hard Water," © Christopher Brown, chrisbrownphotography.com
Author photo: © Rebecca Lawton, beccalawton.com
Cover design: David Provolo
Interior/typesetting design: Rebecca LeGates

Publisher's note: *What I Never Told You: Stories* was originally released as *Steelies and Other Endangered Species: Stories on Water* by Little Curlew Press, LLC, Sarasota, Florida.

Credits

Earlier versions of these stories were published in the following journals and anthologies.

"*An Exposition of the Development of the Earth*" in *Slippage*, Volume 2, February 2014; "Gravity" as "Change of Heart" in *The Acorn: A Journal of the Western Sierra* (El Dorado Writers' Guild, 1995); "The Road to Bonanza" in *Midway Journal* (June 2011, nominated for 2011 Pushcart Prize); "The Middle of a River in Flood," in *Standing Wave* (Elliott Treichel, 1997); "Sandstone" in *THEMA* (THEMA Literary Society, 1995); "Sipapu" in *Milk & Ink: A Mosaic of Motherhood* (Outskirts Press, 2010); "Steelies" in *Connotations* (The Island Institute, 2011); "Only Water" performed by *Page on Stage* (Glaser Center and KRCB Radio 91.1 FM, Sonoma County, 2006); "What I Never Told You" in *Walking the Twilight* (Northland Publishing, 1994); "The Wish" in *Perigee: Publication for the Arts*, Volume 7, Issue 3, April 2010.

For my grandparents

Austin and Marjorie Frost,
R.E. Lawton, Sr., and Jenny Lawton

*who taught me to love and honor nature
and to never abandon art.*

Contents

*Nothing is weaker than water. Yet for overcoming
what is hard and strong, nothing surpasses it.*

—LAO-TZU

WHAT I NEVER TOLD YOU

What I Never Told You

·   ·   ·

You came to the Canyon after the war and left when you had to—years later, when the sons of bitches we worked for let you go. Everybody besides them knew the river was the best place for you, with its sidecanyons and grottoes, maybe the only place a guy could stand to live after two years of hell in a strange jungle. Other vets were going crazy when they came home, never fitting in, sometimes taking a brother or lover with them when they went off. Because what's a man supposed to do, get a desk job? After he's been trained to slit the throats of his sleeping enemies? After he's walked point in utter darkness, developed a sixth sense for trip wires? Even now, though I'm thinking you might have left the river sooner, I can't picture you ever working in some darkened office, eating microwaved meals and staring at a windowless wall. On the river you found your perfect niche.

Damn you anyway. When the cops called that day, I slammed down the phone mid-sentence. I told the one cop he lied, that he didn't know you. Maybe I screamed

at him—I don't know—for being wrong. He didn't get
that you were just out of place. Back on the river there
was room for you. You could live under the sky, use your
knife every day, feel a rush in the biggest rapids. You
could work with ropes, coil them, tie them, pull them and
cut them. You'd wear your boots, those green-and-black
hightops you never took off. Even at night you wore them,
your feet sticking toes down into the sand past the end of
your vinyl groundcloth.

Nights when you fell asleep halfway down the beach
or up in the kitchen, wherever you finished a bottle, I'd
cover you with your blanket. But I wouldn't touch the
boots. You said wearing them around the clock pulled
you through more than one night raid—nasty skirmishes
other foot soldiers never survived.

You had been on the river ten years before I came
there, young, ready for everything. You were the veteran
boatman; I was the eager trainee. You swept like one
more drop of water into the foam and waves and sharp
falls that together pounded loud and thunderous. You'd
spent nights under the dark sky and bright stars, watching the glow on far rims after the moon goes down. You
had the distance in you.

I drew to you as fast as water runs off stone. Who
could've resisted? I had come to the Canyon to learn the
rapids, the names of sidecanyons, the best route through
Lava Falls, how to survive the heat. You knew it all. You
could show me. Since coming home you'd spent every
summer rowing long days against the wind, setting up
camps after dark, and lining up for the bubble line entry
at Lava. You had run all the rapids maybe a hundred
times, mostly nerve ending and mumbled prayer, the
same way you say you walked point. You may have lost

your soul to the war, your youth to an Asian whore, but your heart still beat hot and fast.

At the oars you showed an artist's skill and a madman's flair, detached from fear in a God-given way. To you, the hairball entry at Crystal Rapids was the world's greatest cakewalk, a waltz with another great giant. I could only watch in awe alongside the other members of the crew. But being the only female, my unspoken wonder worked two ways: I knew how your hair curled at the nape of your neck, how you stood tan and tall, all parts intact. I knew about the difference in your eyes, their haunted and startled look. They drew me.

I fought a growing urge to touch you—but what to do with a man who tells scary war stories? When you caught me looking, you blinked, then smiled so dazzlingly wide the hope of every angel crashed in on my heart.

•   •   •

Of all places, we kissed first at the Flagstaff drive-in. Ironic, after what the police said when they called, but true. We had spent all those days and nights on a wild river, leading people through glades of single-leafed ash and cottonwood near clear-running pools. But we never kissed until we huddled on one of those asphalt bumps built up for cars to face the big movie screen.

We had driven out under a striped sky, crimson at the dark earth and lavender up higher, and then indigo under the first spread of stars. Just off the trip and smelling shower-clean, you looked handsome in a pair of new jeans and light summer shirt. I wore a blouse and long skirt. You kept your big hand on my knee, moving only to shift gears. We parked outside the chain-link fence and hoisted up a blanket before we climbed over to the right side of the lot, where only a few cars had parked. We spread the blanket for us and set up a window speaker as nighthawks dipped near lightpoles. Sagebrush and popcorn scent carried on the evening breeze.

You left to fetch snacks as the title, *The Corpse Grinders*, blasted onto the screen. Your laugh reached back to me from the refreshment stand. When you returned, I pulled you to me. We giggled and huddled together as the corpse grinders fed chopped human liver to rampant killer cats.

Soon you lay on and around me, rolling in my arms on the blanket and asphalt, your breath smelling thick of smoke and beer. I kept my mouth open to kiss you. Your hands snaked under my blouse and skirt, your callouses felt rough on my clean skin, breasts, and belly.

"Oh la la," you whispered.

I rubbed your boots with my toes, groped for your jeans, tugged open your fly. Inside were coarse, curled hairs and humid skin. I dug deeper, then pulled my hand away too fast when I felt you. I tried to reach in again, but you rolled away.

"I can't," you cried.

I had guessed that. You'd felt as limp as string. I brushed tiny rocks from your shirt as I cursed the hard ground of the Flagstaff drive-in. Maybe it would have gone better on some beach on the river, in the sand still warm from the summer sun. You sobbed as I covered you in the thin camp blanket—it was yours, government issue.

"Forget it, R.J." You shook your head. You could never have anything normal with me. If you loved me, I would leave you, too.

I got that. You'd already told me about John from Twin Falls, who'd wanted to come home to raise quarter horses. And Henry from Helena, who'd planned to manage his dad's hunting lodge. You'd outlived your whole

squad, all nine men blown away like leaves, not once
but twice. The second time you'd made it by burrowing
under the dead bodies of your buddies until the V.C.
swept through. If I'd pried more, I would have shared
your nightmare: crushed intestines, fixed stares, pumping
blood. Better men than you, you claimed—and here you
were.

The credits rolled as car engines started across the
drive-in. We climbed back over the fence to walk to your
truck, the Chevy El Camino with a rack built of beat-up,
sawn-off oars. We rode back to town, toward crystalline
streetlights in a clear August night. You drove me back to
the boathouse, though I said I'd go with you to Williams,
to anywhere. Maybe we could just drive all night and figure things out. But you dropped me off fast. No wonder
your next words stunned me.

You were in love with me, you said, then pulled the
truck door closed. All stirred up, I watched your taillights move away under the other red lights in town, the
blink-blinking aircraft-warning signals up on the peaks.

· · ·

But try telling all that to the police. Ask anybody, not just
the cops I talked to, to take a heart as big as the world
and give it some shit. Rough it up really good, then turn
it loose and see how it does. Or just watch a star fall, or a
bird blow to earth in a storm.

· · ·

Our little window slammed shut as fast as it had opened,
just as the summer season was ending. September
pressed in. The crew had told me you drank more toward

the end of the season—everybody did as dread crept in about winter jobs and colder weather, but you gave the flasks your full devotion. I knew better than to break up that love affair, even as the nights when I had to cover you grew more frequent. Soon you were falling asleep out of your bag every night, curled up on the beach near a bottle. You were getting harder to wake each morning. The crew sent me to do it, thinking a woman's voice would startle you the least, forgetting how much it would dent my heart to see you huddled alone on the sand.

Flocks of egrets moved upstream, on to somewhere, as fall pushed them upriver. The pairs of ducks we saw didn't linger in pools; no more stopping and starting and letting us chase them downstream on late afternoons. They flew right through the Canyon as I watched you watch the birds move on.

No doubt about it: drink didn't improve your disposition. In that you were no exception. The crew knew to give you room the morning after, but the passengers didn't. And you had to go and mix a hangover with our scheduled day at Havasu Creek. Talk about your worst combination. Havasu was the spookiest place on the river for you, the most reminiscent of the jungle, the only side-canyon so tangled with wild grape and overgrown cottonwood and willow, it put you right back in the war. I'd seen you beside Havasu Creek in a full sweat, first thing in the morning, just remembering. I'd seen you talking to yourself, your face covered with tears, your features twisted. It was the only place I witnessed your dialogue with demons, usually hidden or silent. Maybe if the New York lawyer's wife had snuck up behind you on a good morning at another creek, you'd have kept your job.

I didn't see what happened, but I heard it: twin screams, yours and hers. Later she confessed between sobs that she had run up tippy-toe behind you to tap on your shoulder—you who could hear footsteps or a whisper fifty yards away. But you were lost in the jungle that day. You'd whirled on her—tall in your instant ferocity—spun her and held your knife to her throat. As soon as you did it, you realized your mistake, as soon as the knife pressed to soft flesh. Of the screams I heard, I remember yours, anguished and terrible.

You let her go. She squealed and ran for the boats.

By the time I saw you through the wild grape, your fate had been sealed. First I recognized your boots on the trail, then I saw a man wearing them who was strange to me. You looked crumpled, your sun shirt torn and half-tucked into your cutoffs. You turned to the creek and threw away your knife. It struck a midstream boulder, clattered, and fell into the turquoise water. I opened my mouth to call your name, and you whirled in the path. You stared and swayed, a world away.

I tried but couldn't call your name. My mouth opened and closed, opened and closed, no sound coming out.

You squinted. I waved. Unsmiling, you peered, turned, and lurched into a trailside ocotillo. You weaved and staggered down the path, hobbling out of sight, headed for the boats and the river.

•   •   •

In early December of that year, you started calling me. You didn't reveal much over the telephone, just laughed and said you were fine. You were sure you'd be back on the river next season. Some veteran's program was working wonders, but I never found out where it was. Each time, I asked for your number. Each time, you didn't tell me. Instead you teased, drawing out my name—*Arrr Jay, Arrr Jay*—then hung up the phone.

Once when your voice was clear and strong, you said, "Just remember one thing, R.J.—I'm in love with you," then signed off.

I wanted to whisper sweet words, too, but you were gone before I could, and the line went dead. When you called around Christmas, your voice slurred with drink, I had to sign off. The next call came from the police, who said my number had been in your wallet.

Now I know you had been living in your truck, maybe even since September. The last place you'd had a meal and a shower under one roof may have been back at the boathouse in Flagstaff. It wasn't even the cops who found you. Two guys on a cleanup crew saw you in your locked car after showtime at a drive-in in Bakersfield. They pounded on your window. They shouted at you to "wake up, mister, the movie's been over for an hour." When they couldn't rouse you, they called the police.

The cop read me the coroner's report: adult male, veteran of the Vietnam War. Williams, Arizona, address. Thirty-six years old. Alcoholic seizure. Found in street clothes and combat boots.

The cop said, too, that the coroner was amazed you could wear any kind of shoe. "Pair of wicked bone spurs. Never could have passed selective service."

I told him your feet must've been normal—you'd been drafted. You had not only been called up, you'd served. It was the war that drove you crazy; there was no way you'd been born like that. I told him the truth and slammed down the receiver.

Soon as I did, I picked it up again. There was a lot I could tell them. They didn't know you slept with your boots on, face down mostly, that you worked on the river and could sleep anywhere, even in the cab of your truck. You'd gone cold turkey and were going to work again next season. You had things to look forward to. You were in love with me.

It wasn't a cop's voice I heard then—just dial tone. No words. Just a whine lonelier than silence, lonelier even than a river's hush when winter's coming. Nothing from me, either. Just my mouth opening and closing, opening and closing, no sound coming out.

Sipapu

. . .

True hugged her lover goodbye as the storm blew in. She stared over his shoulder at a flock of blackbirds that settled on a tumbled patch of soil she had just turned for a garden. "Don't worry about me, True," Doug said as he stepped into his pickup. "I'll just be nose to grindstone." With her artist's eye for detail, True observed the first flakes of snow falling as big and soft as rose petals, at first not sticking to earth but instead melting away from the dark brown soil. Gray and low, the overcast sky moved fast, with shrinking views of cobalt blue between the clouds. As Doug started his ignition, the blackbirds scared up to a tree that True hated, a fruitless mulberry on the property line.

The forecast had promised a late-season blizzard, which swept in within hours of Doug's departure. A heavy snowfall closed the mountain road behind him. True paced the house. She knew he wouldn't be in touch until the road reopened. His cell phone barely got reception up at the ski shed, and his company had an emergency-only landline policy during snow-ins. Usually she agreed that not talking during work hours was wise, but this time was different. This time he knew about the test results she had received from the clinic; she'd shared them with him only minutes after seeing them herself.

True moved ghost-like from window to window, looking out. She could have played the radio or watched weather news but didn't. Out front, the faraway peaks where Doug worked were obscured by clouds. In the backyard, the plot of soil so irresistible to blackbirds lay under a foot of powder. Still the snow came. Snowplows growled through the neighborhood but couldn't keep the roads clear.

Nausea stirred her gut. Waves of it had begun not long after her last lovemaking with Doug and had stayed insistent. Why did they call it morning sickness? It was all-the-time sickness—bile on her tongue, inertia in every limb, a vague dizziness. She felt worst when she hadn't eaten, so she devoured salt-water crackers. She couldn't keep up her painting, because the strong smell of the oils repelled her. If she opened the tubes or spent time in their presence, she'd be put off food altogether. She turned her thoughts to escaping with Doug for their planned week away. If they were still going.

She dialed him, phone policy or no, putting the call through the central operator. A machine voice answered at the ski shed. "Hello! You've reached Snow Eagle Adventures. We're out skiing the steep and deep! Please leave a message—" True hung up.

Pulling on pack boots, she went to dig out the driveway and clear off her old Volvo wagon. She bundled up and stepped out the back door, where the chill brought immediate tears. She fought the roiling in her stomach as she scraped the ground with the a shovel blade. Below the snow's titanium-oxide white, asphalt showed the color of graphite—it would make a good study in contrasts. She finished and went inside to rest.

. . .

Doug returned home near dark on the third day, when she was clearing the driveway for the sixth or so time. He drove in without a pause and met her as she replaced the shovel on the back steps. Snowflakes turned to water droplets on his sepia hair and Prussian blue fleece jacket. His eyes looked opaque and rimmed with the raccoon rings he got when he hadn't slept.

"Thank God you're here," he said. "I forgot my key."

"Of course I'm here." She heard the edge in her own voice and didn't say anything about their planned vacation week, meant to start in less than twenty-four hours.

He sighed. "Let's go in."

She knew better than to argue when exhaustion thinned his patience. Another time when he had misplaced his key, she'd hurried back from her gig teaching a sixth-grade class in beginning drawing. She had excused herself from the students as quickly as possible but hadn't wanted to detach too abruptly. After driving the few miles home to let Doug in, they had met on the front porch, where he'd sworn in frustration as the key gave him trouble, then cursed at her when she told him to relax. His words grew hot and personal as she objected, from *pain-in-the-ass* to *bitch* and finally to the C word. She'd packed and driven off to go live with her sister R.J. in Flagstaff, staying away for a month until reluctantly reconciling with a very contrite Doug.

Indoors now, the stuffy air hit her in a wave. She entered as far as the living room while he made two

stops: the bathroom for a voluminous pee and the bedroom to collapse on their queen bed. Within minutes
the sound of his snoring drifted back to where she rested
on the old loveseat. His rattled breathing, sometimes so
endearing, shifted to an annoying *putt-putt-putt*. She felt
bile rise in her throat again. Of course he'd been too tired
to mention the week off, but he had said nothing about
her condition, hadn't asked how she might be feeling.

They'd spoken about it just once, in bed together the
night before the storm. At first their closeness in the
sheets felt warm and easy. He skimmed her body with
a touch as breezy as silken wings, a mere brush that
seemed near and far away at the same time.

"Talk to me," she said. "Say what you're thinking."

He kissed her right eyelid. It stuck shut a few seconds.
"You're beautiful. I love your burnt umber hair and chro-
mium-green eyes." He'd matched them to her oils one
day while she was composing a still life with coffee and
apples.

"But do you want to keep it this time?"

He sighed and rolled away. "Aw, True, I'm still just a kid
myself."

She felt her heart plummet. To return to the special
clinic, to be sucked clean—she didn't think she could face
it again. Tears would run into her ears as she stared at the
ceiling and felt a new hollow space inside her. The last
time, she had known the moment the small life passed
out of her, an instant before the stranger doctor had
leaned to within inches of her face and frowned.

He'd asked, "How will you be more careful in the
future?"

She had promised to use a condom as well as her daily
oral contraceptive.

But Doug had refused. "That's what the damn pills are for."

She had done her weeping in private. Luckily the nomadic R.J. had been home and could keep True company by phone. R.J. had sent roses, too, Mars violet heirlooms.

"Where's Doug?" R.J. had asked.

"On the mountain. Leading a group of heli-skiers from Texas."

R.J., a wilderness guide herself, snorted. "Bastard."

"It's his work, R," True said. "What's he supposed to do, skip it?"

"Why not? I mean, what the hell, T? Since when are the cheap thrills of some rich guys from Houston—"

"San Antonio."

"Whatever. How are they more important than the tiny, precious life growing inside you?"

◆ ◆ ◆

True slipped in beside Doug two hours after his return but startled awake when she noticed he had gone again. She went to the window. Outside the first hint of dawn showed as shards of pale yellow through general overcast. The blanket on his side of the bed was turned down, the steel-gray sheets rumpled. Another shift after three straight nights on the mountain? Unheard of. She moved at a cautious pace through the dim living room, looking for one of his kitchen-table notes. The scrawl on the back of an electric-bill envelope read, "Called back to work—2 a.m.—road closing again."

The driveway showed his departing tracks, pressed-down ruts dotted with fresh, ghost-white pellets of rind snow. The back porch still bore footprints from his driving boots. She pulled her down coat over her winter pajamas, cleared powder from both sets of steps, then returned to the kitchen. A blinking light on the phone machine signaled that a call had come in during her shoveling. She punched the button, eager to hear from Doug.

But it was R.J., calling from the Flagstaff bungalow she rented with another Grand Canyon guide. "Hey, T, are you and Doug still coming down? The futon awaits. Call me!"

Packing didn't take long. In the space below Doug's note, True wrote her own. Short and to the point, she thought. She called her sister back and left a message saying she was on her way. Then she locked up the quiet, unlit house. She backed out of the long driveway over a dusting of new snow, glimpsing the park across the street in her rearview mirror. Moms often pushed their kids in the swings there, but on that morning the play equipment sat frozen and barren.

South of the mountains, she followed roads that stretched clear and dry. High desert lay like a canvas of raw sienna under cerulean blue. True drove all day, musing to herself, not even playing the radio. Before dark she reached the Arizona state line, which she had crossed before but never in winter. Night was on its way, taking forever to fall in the expanse of open country. A billboard showing red-and-orange replicas of The Mittens in Monument Valley read, "Leaving Navajoland." She hadn't been aware of having arrived in it, and no billboard named the land she now entered. Instead, a small wooden sign pointing left simply read "First Mesa" in stenciled letters.

She turned. Beyond a series of washes and valleys, a pale, titanate moon rose from behind an edge of tableland. She drove toward the growing brightness on a rough road that narrowed to one lane hewn in rock. A few signs too dark to read in the moon's backlight stood along the shoulder. She motored past them, topping the mesa near a neighborhood of ancient pueblos.

The road became a mere path between rows of adobe homes. True's car was the only one up there, moving or not. Low-roofed, dark-porched earthen houses threw blocks of night shadow under moonlight, their small windows glowing golden. No streetlights broke the night, but in her headlights True saw a migration of people. There were moving pods of teenagers, arm-in-arm couples, families with small children in tow, fathers holding infants, mothers taking their daughters by the hand—a hushed flow of community. True inched the opposite direction, jostled in her wagon by ruts and sudden potholes, aware that heads turned as she drove by.

Too self-conscious to stop, she continued beyond the village to the edge of the mesa. There she killed the car engine and stared at the incandescent sky. Down below, in the shadow of the mesa, stretched a carbon void. Somewhere there lay a dark desert floor. In her rearview mirror, she saw only the pueblo window-lights and a growing, gold-ochre radiance in the center of the village.

Her body ached. She felt off balance and ill. Too tired to investigate the glow and too curious not to, she unbent herself from the car. People still streamed past the stone buildings, presumably toward the light. She stumbled over the minor rises and falls of a mostly smooth stone surface to join the river of humanity.

A drumbeat pulsed somewhere, growing louder, drawing her to an adobe-walled arena one hundred or so yards in diameter. A bonfire blazed in the center. All around the fire were stadium steps covered by seated people. Other villagers stood behind them in an outside ring, which True joined, the only pale-skinned face she could see in the crowd. They noticed her, she was certain, but their gazes didn't fall on her for long.

The fire's brilliance reached far overhead. On the opposite side of it, an elder kept a steady drumbeat with surprising strength. He wore his long, white hair rolled up and bound with a strip of turquoise cloth—a style she recognized from ancient photographs of indigenous people. Catlike, he crouched in a stance so strong it threatened to launch him from his drum and into the air. He rocked, and the crowd swayed with him.

In a moment a string of men shuffled into view, hands to shoulders chain-gang style. True counted twelve dancers, aged from their teens to perhaps seventies. Their cotton shirts and pants looked soft and home sewn; their turquoise headbands seemed torn from the same cloth as the drummer's. They quickened their step to the beat but even so appeared subdued, as if they'd been dancing all day, or all their lives. Their faces stayed neutral in the open manner of fresh-stretched canvas.

People came and went from the gathering, acknowledged by nods from their neighbors. True watched their easy familiarity with a mix of jealousy and creeping fatigue.

Despite the peace and rhythm of the gathering, she fought nausea. Finally she left the circle, certain that she'd heave the little food she had eaten on the road. Finding a juniper, she bent close and waited. Nothing came. She took in the fragrance of the small, aromatic tree but felt too sick to find it beautiful. She retired to her station wagon, reluctant to leave the fire and safe space among the people. Opening the rear of the station wagon, she rolled out her bedding in the back.

Doug would love it there, she knew, fond as he was of high places. He would pitch the tent near the edge of the mesa, arrange their sleeping bags just so, and make sure they were zipped together and warm. They would talk until their words slurred, about everything they'd seen that day. Then True would curl up against him all night, belly to back, legs drawn up.

Instead she lay alone, planning what she would say when she called him the next morning.

The last time they had conceived, he'd told her, "Things are just taking off for me at Snow Eagle—with a kid, I wouldn't have time to help run the business."

He'd promised her that more financial stability would help quell his anger. He'd been convincing, loving, apologetic for "all the hard times."

"But just remember all the good," he said, and she'd agreed. They could try again later.

That was before she knew how sterile she would feel within the clinic walls and how big a void the vacuum tube would leave. Thinking of it, she kept the rear of the car open to the living heartbeat of drumming from the arena. It lulled her. Eventually the chatter in her mind ceased, allowing a deep, quiet sleep.

. . .

In the morning True awoke to gnawing hunger and a general disorientation. When she saw the sky out every window, mostly first-light blue with a wash of sky blue up higher, she rose feeling wobbly but strong enough to go look for food. Driving back through the village, she was relieved to draw little attention, passing only a woman wearing a Ganado red shawl pulled close against the west wind. True descended the same road she had climbed the night before, observing hand lettering on the road-side signs she'd missed in the dark: "No vehicles past this

point—Hopi Village Cooperative." Hot embarrassment
rose up in her.

At the base of the mesa, she found a small café. She
parked around the side of it, near a small entrance
marked with a simple metal sign: "Hopi Silversmith
Guild." Just past the door stood a glass telephone booth.
She shut herself in it. Dialing, she paused as something
shifted in the pinyon and juniper forest—maybe a large
animal, running, dodging the sagebrush and trees. She
held her breath. Whatever it was headed her way, moving
among the sparse desert foliage until it emerged not ten
feet from the booth.

A young man, naked to the waist and with face and
torso gessoed white, darted past her. He wore a long
loincloth over skin pants and a beaded sash that whipped
with his stride. His black, blunt-cut hair was held in a
turquoise headband, again like those worn by the dancers and drummer the night before. As the runner disappeared through the door to the guild, True spotted his
scarlet athletic shoes with crisp neon-green logos.

She hung up the phone just as the answering machine
clicked on. Leaving the booth, she followed the runner
inside, jostling a rack of bells over the door. An immediate flood of heat from a fireplace across the room
enveloped her. There was no sign of the running spirit. A
middle-aged Hopi man with black-and-silver hair stood
in an island of glass jewelry cases, wiping the counter
with a white cloth.

"Good morning!" He smiled. "How are you today?"

"Dizzy." She staggered toward him. "I just need . . ." A
soft couch provided a landing for her heavy fall.

• • •

True woke to the sight of four heads hovering above her. Had she been sleeping? No, she figured, she'd passed on and was witnessing a welcoming party of loved ones who'd gone before. Her great-grandmother Truella, her Grandma Betsy and Grandpa Ed, her childhood dogs Benjamin and Freckles. But wait—the faces came into focus. They weren't relatives and long-deceased pets. They were strangers, their cheeks burnished with the glow of wind and sun. Among them was the first man, who had greeted her from behind the jewelry counter.

"She's coming to," said a massive tribal policeman in sunglasses and dress uniform. A radio receiver crackled on his belt.

"Move back and give her air," the jewelry man said.

A woman in a Ganado red shawl—the same one True had seen on the road?—commanded, "Johnny, go ask Cook for a Number Three plate. And water. Bring water."

One of the faces departed, the one that hadn't yet spoken. It belonged to the youngest of them by far—teenager, probably—with wide eyes and combed-back hair still wet from showering.

The red-shawl woman said her name was Louise.

True whispered, "I'm Truella. Or True."

"Beautiful. Family name?"

True nodded.

Louise smiled, her teeth white and even. "I'm named for ancestors, too. I have their clan name: Sun Clan."

In spite of wanting to hear more, True let her eyes close. She didn't open them again until the smell of fried meat and burnt sage woke her from another nap. The faces were gone, but a T.V. tray sat before her, laden with breakfast. In a rush, she consumed it all—blue corn pancakes with syrup, a generous serving of sausage, two glasses of fruit juice. Soon her gut felt full and at peace. She finished breakfast and rose to her feet to stretch.

Wandering to the silversmith's part of the room, she admired an array of silver bracelets and necklaces under glass in velvet-lined trays. The jewelry man worked behind his counter, writing on a notepad.

"Thank you for helping me," she said. "I haven't been well."

He looked up. "Not everyone feels okay all nine months."

True's cheeks flushed.

"No shame. Louise went through it five times."

True raised fingers to the face she guessed had deepened to quinacridone pink.

"Don't worry." He reached out a hand. "Every time, she told me it was worth it. I'm Henry. Where are you from?"

She shook the offered hand. "Utah. South of Salt Lake City."

"Your husband isn't with you?"

"We're . . . not married." She kept her eyes down. "He's working."

"Ah." Henry released her fingers and pulled a bracelet from behind glass. "Look at this." He ran a finger along the overlay design in the band, charcoal-colored concentric circles in brilliant silver, the curves opening on one side. A many-legged figure stood in the center of the labyrinth.

"This is a *kiva*," Henry said. "It means both Home and Place of Emergence."

"Emergence?"

"Creation. Birth. Our elders say we entered this world by way of the first kiva, the *sipapu*. Three worlds before this one failed."

"What went wrong?"

Henry lowered his voice. "Same old, same old. Arguing. They couldn't work things out. Our people decided to start over, so they followed Spider Grandmother up through the sipapu into a better world." He tapped the figure on the bracelet.

True nodded. "I've heard about the sipapu. From my sister, R.J. She works on the Colorado River in the summer."

"It's a sacred place."

In a moment the wide-eyed youth returned, carrying a pitcher of water. "Dad? Mom's busy in the café but reminded me to bring this."

"My son Johnny," said Henry. "He's my youngest. Just finishing high school."

Johnny left the pitcher with his father and turned to go. Maroon letters across the back of his white T-shirt read, "Flagstaff 20K. Peak to Creek Challenge."

"He's still growing," said Henry, pouring a paper cup full of water. "Luckily he's found the Running Way. Got first in his age group in that Flagstaff race last month. He's learning the old dances, too—learning patience. He'll need it when he has a family of his own."

Johnny waved away his father's words as if swatting a fly.

Henry shrugged. "It's the truth."

Johnny rolled his eyes and left the room. As he did, True looked for running shoes on his feet. They were bare.

As Henry put away the kiva bracelet and slid the case closed, True felt her heart yearn for the sipapu.

Henry smiled, his eyes steady. "Johnny says he's too young to think about having a family. Maybe so. But our children are why we live. Even when they give us trouble. Take Johnny. Louise and I thought we were going to lose him a few years back. He went off with some so-called friends, not from the village. I think he wandered far from the mesas. Maybe even got into drugs."

"You don't know?"

He shook his head.

"Drove us nuts, not knowing. We wondered why we ever had a son, too much heartache and worry. Then Johnny took up running. Maybe to impress some girl? Anyway, next he found the dances—rain dance, snake dance, clown dance, corn dance. All of them. Anything to do with the tribe and our clan he got into in a big way."

The jewelry and trays blurred in True's sight. "Earrings," she murmured. "Can you show me some earrings, Henry?"

"Sure." His fingers went straight to a pair of posts with matched black curls on disks smaller than dimes. "Here. These are our symbol for water. Waves for flowing around anything in your path. Water is very female. Strong and wise."

He urged True to put them on, then set a mirror in front of her. She started at the sight of her pale, tired face, but tried to focus on the earrings, which shone with simple integrity. Something to aspire to.

"Beautiful," she said. "You made them?"

"No. Cecilia did, my oldest daughter. She's getting good—she'll keep the Sun Clan work going long after I'm gone."

"I'll take them. And another pair for my sister R.J."

He agreed, though he warned that R.J. should not wear them on the river. "If she does, she'll lose them."

"But they'll still protect the wearer if she leaves them home?" True thought of her own tendency to forget earrings back in the modest jewelry case beside her bathroom sink.

Henry nodded. "From this day forward."

. . .

True dialed the telephone in the chilly booth outside the guild. Static ticked in the lines that crossed the hushed desert and mountain passes she had driven alone.

Doug answered. "Hello?"

She opened her mouth to speak, but no words came.

"Anyone there?" he asked.

Her exhaled breath made small white clouds as her heartbeat drummed in her ear.

"Christ," he muttered. "True, is that you?"

A chain of narrow highways stretched from the open land surrounding her toward the kitchen from which he must be gazing out toward his jagged peaks.

"Yes," she said at last. "Yes, it's me. Me and my baby."

She returned the receiver to its cradle. Exhaling, she steadied herself against the glass beside her.

In the bright morning, the desert looked calm, endless. She stepped away from the shadow of the guild. As she crossed the parking lot, she felt strong and wise, patient enough to flow on her path. She slid in behind the wheel of her wagon and started the engine. She drove south, through a valley where two farmers bent to their hoes in a cadmium red field. Crossing a trickle of water that glinted in a sandy wash, she made her way up and above it. Downshifting to climb the steepening slope, she continued on the ramp of road toward open sky.

Seven Pieces of Pineapple

. . .

June 8
Flagstaff, Arizona

Trip arrived here a half day before I did. I thought he'd be under his truck in Angels Camp forever and arrive later. But I pulled in after sundown and found his blue-black pickup (with new clutch now, I guess) already lined up with some other cars near the warehouse. His kayak hung out the back like a big board of lumber.

I tossed my groundcloth and bag under a pine in the middle of the yard to claim a sleeping spot. Just then Trip walked up. He told me the boatmen were in the house.

"Let's knock on the door, Mare," he said.

I was beat but said okay.

Jimmy, the manager, opened the door a crack. Out poured light and heat. We were dying to go inside and sit by the woodstove. It's chilly here, six thousand feet in the air. Hard to believe we're so near the Grand Canyon, the mile-deep furnace.

Trip tried to slip in the door, me behind him. I saw one of the boatmen—sunburned cheeks, shoulder-length hair, bandanna headband. A smile warm as the woodstove. I smiled back. But Jimmy did not smile. He told us to come back later, after they'd debriefed the latest river trip.

Outside, Trip swore and pulled out a smoke. "How's it feel to be a flunky, Mare?"

"Different. Who'd you see in there?"

"Dave. Wesley. Bryce. Big Dan."

"Wow. The legends."

"Yeah. The goddamn elite." Trip laughed his wicked laugh.

"What about that guide named R.J.?"

"Nope, no women."

With the cigarette on his lips he tossed his kayak out of the truckbed so he could sleep back there. He didn't ask me to join him—finally taking no for an answer? I headed for my pine tree and sleeping bag.

Trip got here by driving straight through, stopping only in Vegas to play blackjack. I came by way of Owens Valley. Sagebrush, mountains east and west, gray swath of highway. Hot, eye-watering winds. Outside Bishop I gassed up at an old station with two rusty pumps.

Some people were gathered at the empty lot next door while the Inyo County sheriff looked on. He told me they were filming a Western. "Andy Griffith is the star. Hang around, you can probably meet him."

"No thanks. I'm trying to beat a friend to Arizona."

"Some friend." He looked inside my VW. "I wish I had a beautiful woman like you who can drive. And a stick shift at that."

His big gold wedding ring caught my eye. "Your wife can't drive?"

"No way. She lost her nerve years ago." Now he does all the driving for both of them.

I continued on—first to Flagstaff to meet Trip and pick up some river gear, then to Utah in convoy with him for our river season. My VW shuddered with every passing truck, made worse by the kayak on my roof. I had to stop a couple times to steady myself. No wonder, then, that Trip got to Arizona first.

• • •

June 9
Flagstaff

This a.m., up at dawn. Still ungodly cold. I walked a dirt road to the prairie to look for black antelope. The boatmen said you can spot them out with the light ones, running in herds. Black antelope are rare—you have to be patient to see them. Red soil, yellow pine forest. I saw no antelope of any color before hunger pangs hit.

BREAKFAST
granola
raisins
almonds

have bowl
need spoon
need milk

Heading back I stopped at a small house with a sign advertising fresh milk. I knocked and met a lady who keeps cows. She wore an old dress and sweater, had only a few teeth. Her husband sat in a wheelchair watching

TV. Some people called the Johnson Sisters were singing about having a friend in Jesus. The husband grinned at me and nodded. Can't speak much, it seems.

He's a shut-in but the wife gets out. She takes a truck and chainsaw to the mountains when they need firewood. She doesn't see the black antelope "but once or twice a year."

Their house sits right on the Santa Fe lines. Trains shriek by day and night. In the middle of our talking, a freight screamed past. The wife stopped mid sentence and smiled as twenty or more boxcars rumbled by. Then she started right back up, asking about the Grand Canyon and the Colorado.

I told her it's got big water but I haven't been down it yet.

She grew up in Salmon, Idaho, by the Lemhi River. "It's shallow all summer, full of these rocks." She held up a jar crammed with round river stones. All sizes, all colors. "I was like you back in my twenties. Big blue eyes. Blonde hair, too—but mine was long, down my back."

She asked me to bring her more stones from the river. "Any river," she said.

How she keeps herself from hopping a freight out of there I don't know.

Back at the warehouse, Trip was hanging with the Canyon boatmen. They thanked me when I set down the milk. We all stood around eating cereal from plastic mugs. Bryce asked about boating in Utah.

I told him I hear it has beautiful canyons but I haven't been in them yet.

"You'll get there," said Big Dan, who asked Trip, "By the way, how'd you get your nickname?"

I answered. "He fell over the port-a-potty one night last summer."

The boatmen roared.

Trip glared at me over his cigarette smoke. "I'd *had* too many beers." Like that was better than just not seeing it in the dark.

We helped the boatmen load gear for Lee's Ferry. Wesley was binding the ends of some tie straps, so Trip pulled out a Bic lighter to heat-seal them one at a time. Seeing it would take forever, I opened up a cookstove and portable propane and sealed a half-dozen straps at once. The boatmen stopped what they were doing to watch until Jimmy the manager showed up and told them to get back to work.

Now the river truck is loaded with rafts, oars, lifejackets, and food boxes for 14 days on the water. Tomorrow we'll convoy up to Lee's Ferry at dawn. The Canyon boatmen will ride in the truck, Trip will haul the raft and other gear we came for, and I'll drive my VW with Trip's kayak tied next to mine.

Detouring to the Ferry was his idea. He wants to "get in good with the GC boatmen" so they'll ask him to work down here. Bad idea, I said. We have to pack out the first Green River trip day after tomorrow.

He said, "No sweat. We can drive straight through. Remember who won the race to Arizona."

DINNER
peanut butter
no jam
potato bread
green apple
oatmeal cookies (6)

•   •   •

June 10
Lee's Ferry, Arizona

Spectacular! Or should I say Grand? Today the water in
the Colorado is a startling, teal-wing blue. Contrasted
with purple and pink cliffs to the north and — wow! I
get it. I could see working here forever, even though the
Lee's Ferry boatramp is mobbed, the rafts are heavy (one
ton unloaded), and everything's so hot in the sun you
can't touch it. The boatmen move their gear with channel locks, including these *mondo* chains and angle iron
on thick plywood decking that would be overkill on a
smaller river. All on a stretch of pavement the size of a
Kmart parking lot.

Trip and I helped the boatmen pull all the heavy stuff
around. It was insane. I had an idea and told Trip, "I'll
lend the boatmen my kayaking gloves. They'd work better
than their crazy channel locks."

"Right." Trip grabbed my gloves. "I'll take those to
Dave."

Trip was back with the crew in a flash. Typical. My
idea, my gloves, and Trip taking credit. In a huff I pulled
my kayak down from the VW and paddled upstream
toward Glen Canyon Dam. The river is slow up there and
quiet, a good place to think. I stopped on a large chunk of
rock in a stretch where big domed couches of sandstone
reach between river and sky. Six snowy egrets. Handful of
ravens flew past in a burst—raucous!

I calmed down and fell asleep on the warm rock. After
the sun dropped behind the cliffs, I woke up and paddled
back to the ramp. The boatmen were standing around
Trip and slapping him on the back. He had on my gloves.
The others were wearing those white cotton ones like you
get at Ace Hardware.

"Hey, Mare," Wesley said. "Your friend here saved our asses."

When Trip had showed Dave my gloves, the other boatmen remembered the cotton ones Jimmy had bought them for rowing.

"Great idea." I glared at Trip.

He narrowed his eyes back at me. I wanted to whack him with my kayak paddle but knew that would only make me look bad. Instead I asked for my gloves back. He made a big show of taking them off and returning them to me like I was the jerk here.

The boat ramp quieted down for the night. Rafts from other companies were lined up along shore. Boatmen spread out to the campsites to cook their dinners. Bryce told me two hundred people will launch from here tomorrow. Most will go in motor-powered rafts, huge Army-surplus pontoons that make even our oversized oarboats look tiny.

River gods help me—I want this place.

.   .   .

Same day. Midnight.

Writing by flashlight. After rigging, the boatmen ate a steak dinner courtesy of Jimmy and his chain-smoking assistant Bob. They'd arrived at the boat ramp to help after the hardest work was done. Dark was coming. A single great blue heron flew by with silent wings. Trip and the crew huddled in crumpled poses like the truly tired. Jimmy asked Trip to share in their dinner because he'd helped *so much* with the glove idea. Fine. I put my kayak back up on my VW and got out the makings for a peanut-butter sandwich. Head boatman Dave called me over for dinner.

"There's plenty," he said.

And there was. What a spread: steak, rolls, salad, corn on the cob, fresh pineapple. I went over and dug in.

Jimmy and his sidekick Bob sat off to one side, talking. Bob puffed on a cigarette the whole time. Jimmy watched me as I licked pineapple juice from my fingers. Next thing I knew, he pulled me aside.

"You know, Mary," he said. "You were welcome to the dinner."

"It's Mare. Thanks, it was great—"

"But there were only *seven* pieces of pineapple. Just enough for the main crew, Trip, and Bob and I."

He had to be kidding. I smiled. But Jimmy did not smile. Trip was eating pineapple across from me, looking worried. Thinking I was beating his time with the Arizona boss?

"So what should I do?" I asked Jimmy. "Cough it up?"

He stormed away and drove off in a van with Bob the cigarette puffer. Where to? To report me to the rangers? When the boatmen figured he'd left for the night, they came alive, congratulating me for getting rid of Jimmy. They passed around a box of wine marked Day 12 in black felt-tip pen. A few swigs and I felt a hand on my arm. Big Dan feeling my biceps!

"Keep rowing, Mare," he said. "You'll get hired here."

Trip snorted. "She'd have to be stronger than that."

Bryce laughed and lifted his own skinny arms. "It's not about muscles. We have one woman, R.J., who does it with smarts."

Dave said I should try for it. "The Canyon's the best."

BEST
rapids: Lava Falls (says Bryce)
sidecanyon: Havasu Creek (Dave)
mudbaths: the Little Colorado (Wesley)
wall: Nankoweap (Big Dan)
sunsets: West rim (all)

The boatmen went on: the longest trips, the most money, the best river, the funnest rapids. All the women you could ever want, or men in my case. And parties every night.

We raised our cups. "Every night!"

Later I headed for the restrooms and Trip followed. Maybe to ask for the thing I'll never give him? But he said, "I am *going* to get hired here."

"Me, too."

"You?" He laughed and went around to the men's side.

Women *are* scarce here. But I have to go for it. Otherwise, you know what they'll say. Same as the poor sheriff's wife: she lost her nerve years ago.

• • •

June 11
Vernal, Utah

Lordy, lordy. What a day—ten hours of convoying behind Trip's truck to Utah. Now in the Vernal KOA, surrounded by horse trailers and pickups. There's a rodeo this week. Aspiring cowboys on the road with their parents. We're drained and making obnoxious jokes. We have to get some sleep before packing for the Green tomorrow a.m.

<u>BREAKFAST</u>
Cheerios
milk
bananas (2)

My first views of Utah: rock walls, little stream valleys, aspen, cottonwood, fir. Who would've guessed? Big conifers on the ridges. We sped by. Trip insisted on stopping at Texacos—he says his truck only likes their gas. At the Panguitch Texaco we lunched on sandwiches and watched the locals.

"Something not to be missed," said Trip.

Man on a bay mare in front of Smith's supermarket, talking to a smiling cop. Kid with a 1950s brush cut, holding pop bottles, waiting to cross the highway. High-school girls with pigtails in plastic ball ties, running from their car to the store.

"I'll be damned." Trip sucked on a cigarette. "Must've crossed a time warp at the Arizona line."

Arizona, Arizona—too bad things went bad with Jimmy in the end.

• • •

June 12
Vernal, Utah

<u>RIVER FRUIT SALAD</u>
10 apples
6 apricots
6 peaches
grapes for 22
canned pineapple

This a.m., writing out shopping lists for the Green River. Good to be back at work but hard to be so far from my dream: rowing the Colorado farther downstream. No sooner did I think that than a long-distance call came from Jimmy saying one spot is opening up on the Grand Canyon crew. He asked Trip to transfer down there. My heart dropped about three feet.

Trip noticed. "Give up, Mare. You might as well settle in up here."

"And why is that?"

"You know you'll never get hired in GC. The water's too big for you. The boats are too heavy. And you didn't exactly hit it off with Jimmy."

That's all supposed to stop me?

RIVER FIRE BOX
charcoal & lighter fluid
oil
black pepper
strike-anywhere matches

Hot day in Vernal. Cars creeping by on Main. Men in jeans, cowboy hats, and long-sleeved shirts even in the heat. Maybe not so hot to them, born and raised here? Boatmen from other companies walk by in shorts and t-shirts, ammo boxes in their hands, buck knives strapped on their belts. "Beehive State" (for industry) on every license plate.

We packed rocket boxes in the grocery store parking lot. Trip came across the fruit I'd bought for the fourth night's salad. "What gives with all the pineapple, Mare? Ten cans? Three would be plenty."

"We won't want for pineapple on this trip."

Trip's been talking up the Canyon to the Utah boat-men. They barely listen. On the way to put-in, Miles read a paperback and Snake, who was driving, said he likes it here.

Trip laughed. "Not me. I'm going to transfer to the Canyon faster than you can say 'Jack Mormon.'"

Acres and acres of alfalfa in the valley. Land fenced for quarter horses. Thunderheads blooming over the mountains, sego lilies flowering in carpets of white. We crossed little creeks and farm ditches and almost got to the river before we blew a tire.

Snake pulled over. Miles and Trip blocked the wheels and jacked up the right rear of the van. Frozen lug nuts. Across the highway was a little garage. I went in. I bought soda from a vending machine and borrowed a can of WD-40 from the mother of the mechanic.

She asked about the rivers we ran. I said I'd heard they were wild but hadn't been on them yet.

Back at the van, Miles sprayed the lugnuts with WD-40. They came right off. Good thing—Trip was already red in the face from trying to loosen a couple.

The air smelled sweet from new things growing. I bent down to pick up an old river stone, round and white, half the size of my fist. It shone like a mirror when I rubbed it clean. Opal? I'm keeping it for the woman in Flagstaff until I can get back there.

With the tire changed, we crossed the bridge over the Green. Swallows dipped near the water. A wedge of geese passed overhead. Heading south? If so they'll get to the Canyon before me. But I'll keep rowing, like Big Dan said. Maybe I'll get there slow because it's a man's club and Jimmy doesn't want me. But all paths lead downstream when you follow the river every day. That, and when guys like Trip tell you to settle in.

The Middle of a River in Flood

. . .

If Gwen could see the river tonight, she'd know it's not wild and rising hard, like that day ten years ago. No, the water below Half Moon Bar is smoother than a polished stream cobble. When the river's quiet like this, you can believe trees never slide by, big and torn up, rocks still in their roots. You can imagine the whole old flight of steps leading to the lodge never has to be pulled up above the banks and folded like a ladder above the highest-water mark so it won't wash away in the unruly river. Tonight the water looks tame, reflecting a big moon. The breeze up the canyon smells fresh and clear, not thick with mud, the way it smelled the time we tried to run the river in flood.

Gwen of all people would love the peace here tonight. When I got back after her memorial today, I chopped wood until dark, bit by bit splitting the oak rounds that remained from last year. As I worked, I thought of her lying there in the hospital, how weak and shrunk up she had gotten. Damn, the doctors—did they do any good?

Seems their treatment amounted to no more than bailing a big river with a little bucket. The cancer left nothing, barely enough to bury.

Near the end of my wood-chopping, when I was tired but still swinging hard, sending chips flying, I missed the splitting stump and just grazed my left boot. That scared the hell out of me, so I had to take a break. I walked down to the water to sit on the steps until I stopped shaking. I pictured the younger Gwen, her face when she finally knew we were in trouble. Then later, when we were both out in the water struggling to catch air.

That morning of our river run, she and I drove to the boat ramp in the dark. She was the girlfriend of Ryan, Half Moon Bar's caretaker, and she wanted a lift downstream to see him. She trusted me to be the one to take her.

"He says you're the best, R.J.," Gwen had said, when she first called to ask for a ride.

"Thanks." I did have the years at it, on rivers all over the West. "Tell him thanks from me and I'm happy to row you."

As we followed the river road to put-in, Gwen noticed the madrones in our headlights, wet from the weeklong rains. "What's that shimmering?" she asked.

I leaned close to the windshield and looked up. "You mean the madrone leaves?"

"Yes! That's it—all silver in the lights. They're beautiful, R.J. Magical."

Gwen's green eyes glowed like the undersides of the leaves. Her face looked pale and bright, a headlight of its own. She fixed on the trees as she held a thermos cup of hot tea in her small, pale hands. They were wrinkled and years older than the smooth skin of her young-woman face. She turned her startling eyes toward me again. "I see why you and Ryan love it here. It's gorgeous."

We were towing my brand-new driftboat. I had painted it up in town myself—four coats of sky-blue paint on the wooden hull, black trim on the sideboards, hand-lettered name on the stern, *Sayonara Too*. I'd never even fished from the boat; it was that new to me. I had bought it to enlarge my fleet that for years had consisted of a single aluminum driftboat, *Sayonara One*. A pair of newly varnished ash oars fitted to brass alloy locks completed the *Too*, perfect for chasing down salmon and steelhead and running guests to the lodge. Getting to Half Moon would be a breeze in that rig.

When we arrived at the Grave Creek boat ramp, the river looked higher than the phone report had said. Feeder creeks and side streams must have still been pumping in runoff that the depth gauge in town hadn't measured. Gwen and I stood at water's edge, in our slickers and woolies and milking boots, and watched the muddy flow.

The river looked manageable, but she put her finger on the strangest thing about it.

"There's no one here. Do you think we'll have the river to ourselves?"

"No," I said. "We're just early. Someone's bound to launch later."

"It's fantastic—all wild and empty."

In truth, I'd never been alone at that boat ramp, no matter what the hour or weather.

Gwen seemed to read my doubts creeping in. "Ryan told me you're the only one to ride with in high water."

I nodded. It was true: big water had become my specialty. Plus most of the rapids would be washed out. We could do it.

We backed the trailer down to the shore, though we didn't have to back it very far, because the river covered half the ramp. Then we lined the *Too* into an eddy, loaded a bit of gear for overnighting at Half Moon, and parked the truck and trailer farther up in the big lot. I gave Gwen the standard safety talk—lifevests tight, throw line ready—then took the oars. We kicked off from land and whipped into the current like a leaf in the wind.

Gwen sat up front, braced on the gunnels with her mittened hands. The river surged down the middle in one good set of standing waves. High water covered most of the rocks I used as guides to water level. From time to time she looked back at me, smiling and big-eyed. Sometimes surprise side rollers hit the boat in the belly or caught the sharp rails at the bottom, a feeling I never liked much considering how easily those driftboats flip.

But Gwen didn't know—she just laughed. "Is it always this exciting?"

"Not always."

"But it is now. The river's alive!"

About two miles down from Grave Creek, the rain started again. Gwen noticed something strange—all the tributaries pumping in murky water from the side canyons.

"What's different about the creeks?" she asked. "They're not muddy like the river. They look like tea. Or coffee."

Dark, leaf-stained water poured from gullies and swirled into the foamy current. With the ground already soaked up, little canyons normally choked with gooseberry and fir flushed and spilled that darker color. Most hadn't run that hard in years. Scary to me now, the thought of the creeks churning in from places we couldn't see. Back then, though, I didn't think. I just struggled like mad to control the boat.

The huge falls at Rainie had washed out, an easy channel of small waves. That was no sweat, although it spooked me to glide over a ledge of rock, normally so tall above the river, buried under tons of water. At Horseshoe Bend, the current shot out like water from a firehose through that U-shaped curve, then climbed the bank as far as I've heard it does when the gauge reads twenty feet. If so, it was more than twice as high as had been reported that morning. And in Mule Creek Canyon, the river reached clear to the top of the gorge: surging, pushing, roiling up in boils.

I'd have given my spare oars to know the gauge reading then, though it would have just been a number. It wouldn't have helped us get downstream. Suffice it to say it was higher than I'd ever seen, higher by far than anyone runs solo.

I didn't say anything to Gwen, so of course she got me for being quiet.

"Everything okay, captain?" she asked.

I didn't answer. I was listening.

"R.J.—"

"Shh."

She turned to me, surprised. Then the question left her face, because she heard something, too. Something like a train coming from a long distance, or a jet thundering. Or every last bear out in the woods growling. But it wasn't any of those things. I knew what it was—rapids. Big rapids. Above a certain size they lose their friendlier white noise and take to roaring. Maybe they become all water and no air, and the rumble fills the sky and shakes your ears and heart. The sound meant that downstream, not quite around another bend, was some big whitewater. Blossom Bar in flood.

Gwen looked startled, maybe because there was nothing to see. Blossom bellowed below us, but just the lip of it showed. I could guess what was down there: crashing whitewater filling the rock garden and covering the marker boulders so they were just muddy humps. From up top, we could only see a bowed surface of river rolling ahead.

The only thing to do was pull to shore. I rowed so hard to get over, I almost overshot a little rock cove I was aiming for in the right bank. We made it in, though, and I pulled close to a cliff where we moored the boat. My hands shook as I tied up the bowline while Gwen waited. Then we kind of tiptoed downstream to scout the run.

"Good God," I said when I saw it.

The rapids looked huge and ugly. The usual house-sized boulders were under water, and they made nasty reversals that kicked up froth and spit like I'd never seen before on this river. The standard run, where you swing wide to the left and cut back hard right, was not the usual highway. Not nearly so. Rowing the normal route would mean pulling through some intense, bucking water and around two mean sucking holes.

Gwen watched me as I watched the rapids. "Why's this so much worse than everything else?"

"Blossom's got the biggest rocks on the river, for some reason."

She thought a moment, then asked the million-dollar question. "Can we do it?"

"Well, I've run stuff this bad before," I said. But I never had when there wasn't another boater waiting downstream to pick me up.

She kept looking at me, just waiting, I guess.

"We could walk from here," I said. "It's only two miles to the lodge."

But we were on the wrong side of the river—we would have to line the boat back upstream about a half mile before rowing across. The thought scared me: two of us lining there, with all the fast current and slippery rock.

"Or." I scratched my head. "We could hike this side out to the road." Ten miles along the river path. There'd be no way to make it before dark.

"What should we do?" Gwen asked.

Her face was bunched up with worry, and I wanted her to stop looking that way. I thought of the *Too*, so pretty, bucking at its mooring upstream. Overnight like that, it might bash up. At least if we made it through the rapids and got to Half Moon, Ryan would lower the steps for us. We could secure the *Too* with guy-lines and rest easy in warm beds.

"Let's try it," I said. "It's just two good pulls."

Her face lit up. "I'm in."

I checked the straps on her lifejacket. "Remember. Keep your feet downstream if we land in the river."

She nodded, her eyes wide.

I peeled off my heavy clothes, a habit I'd picked up on trips running big rapids, but decided to keep on my rubber boots. Gwen chose not to strip down—she was cold enough already, she said. She just sat on her haunches on shore, one hand holding the bowline, waiting for the signal. I stepped into the boat. From my seat at the oars, I listened to the river's roar and strained to see my entry into the spray, shock waves, and foam.

"Okay, Gwen!"

She stepped into the bow, carrying the line with her. Again we swept off with the current.

I rowed left with everything I had, reaching far ahead of me, finishing each stroke with my legs. She watched downstream, her hands gripping the gunnels. I made the quickest, strongest strokes possible, arching all the way up as I pulled, recovering as fast as I could. Even so we only reached mid-river by the top of the rapids. The current was just too much for me—something I hadn't felt before, not even earlier that day. As we closed in on the lip of the falls, she got a good look downstream.

She turned and screamed, "Pull, pull!"

The big pyramid rock loomed to our left, just a tip of granite in a huge mound of brown water. We made a last-minute punt and ran a chute between the pyramid and the gorilla-faced rock. Dropping over a little falls, the boat made a sickening, scraping sound. Still, we landed straight, even though it was a hard fall that popped the oars from their locks.

"Shit." I slammed the oars back in place.

Gwen still held the gunnels. "We're okay! Pull! Pull!"

I pivoted to the best angle I could and rowed, but the upstream rail of the boat caught in a surge. We washed down toward the Volkswagen rock, just a monster mid-stream hole at that water level. The *Too* spun nose first into the hole and stopped, but only for an instant before shuddering, snaking up, and twisting over on top of us.

• • •

I've always thought that life's like the river, but anybody can see that. There are backwaters and shallows, bridges and dams. There are smooth parts and rough parts. Like Gwen's illness, years after the river run—that was a rough part. When she lay there, in the medical center that had held out all kinds of hope, I asked her.

"What's it feel like, Gwen? A bad swim?"

Her skin was so pale, I could see into her. And her bright green eyes had turned golden and keen, maybe from the pain, maybe from morphine. She thought about it, her face bunched up.

I asked, "Does it feel like you're drowning?"

"No," she whispered. "Much worse. Stronger." She fell asleep, and as usual I sat with her until she woke up.

She meant worse than feeling a wooden boat crash down on your back in the middle of a river in flood. She meant stronger than being sucked straight down by the water in your boots—worse than staying under so long and tumbling around so much you doubt you'll see daylight again. Or worse than swallowing enough water to make you heave, with no one coming to save you.

Gwen's swim was bad, worse than mine, maybe because she'd kept on her heavy wool clothes. When my boots finally tugged off and I shot to the surface for air, I saw her floating low and fast. The gap between us grew wider with every second. Soon, speeding ahead like that, she'd be swept out of sight.

I swam as hard as I could to get her. When I caught up, it was only because she was stuck in whirlpools along an eddy fence, wheeling like a spinner cast out for trout. She churned the surface with her arms, looking too weak and lost to find shore. Her nose was red, and her hair covered her eyes.

"Swim, Gwen! This way!"

As I reached for her, she looked around but not far enough to see me. A current shot her back out into the river.

No. I couldn't go out there again. I wasn't strong enough to get her.

Then I saw it—an oar sliding by, fast and sleek, out in the river. It looked so streamlined that I knew what to do. Pushing out and swimming low and hard, I told myself to go like the oar. I strained and shoved and broke through each wave, never taking the long ride over the tops but slicing straight through them, just like a ten-foot, solid-ash oar.

Gwen's head showed up downstream past dozens of curlers. When I closed in again, she was swirling on the eddy fence of another backwater, floating even lower than before, swallowing water. Then the swift current headed upstream caught her.

"Gwen! No!" She was about to wash out the top of the eddy.

But I got her. With my right hand, I grabbed for her lifejacket, pulling her back from the whirlpools and main current. With my left I reached for shore, catching something thin and tough hanging from the muddy bank. It was a tree root, sweeping along in the water—sticking down into the current where soil had washed away. It didn't feel like much, but it was enough.

I dragged us over and helped Gwen struggle up the steep bank. Out of the water, we huddled together on a little patch of slicked-down grass, gasping and coughing. When I looked up, I saw the *Too* across the river, just passing the surging eddy below Half Moon Bar. I could only stare. The boat looked like a big fish come to surface, turning in the current, heading fast toward Four Mile Canyon. I had to sit and watch my prize roll out of sight when I wanted so much to run along after it, to do something, anything. But I sat next to Gwen, holding her hand, and didn't move.

"Thanks, R.J. You saved me."

"The hell I did. I about killed you."

"No, you saved my life, so let me thank you."

"Okay."

"Thank you."

• • •

The river looks peaceful tonight. When it's like this, I can forget how it rises up sometimes, brown and pushy. Half Moon's steps are lowered to the water, easy to reach. But on that day, the lodge might've been on Pluto for how hard it was to get to. Across the river, not far from where I pulled Gwen out, there are trees on the bank—Doug-fir, big-leaf maple, madrones—with their roots hanging down. Even the longest of those is far from the water, of course, with the river so low.

Gwen and Ryan split up years ago, and he moved to town. After he left, the new lodge owners still hired me to help around the place. It got tough to stay and care-take the grounds when I was making so many trips to the hospital to visit Gwen. But in her last few weeks, I didn't think much of the lodge during the hours and hours, and days and days, when I sat holding her old, wrinkled hands. Her veins by then were easy to see, the streams of needle marks following her blood lines. She'd collected more different-colored bruises than I'd ever seen, even on people who'd broken bones or taken bad falls.

I hoped like hell that if I held her hand long enough, or just right, she would have cause to thank me again. But of course it didn't go that way, and in the end all her words were gone.

Tonight I could sit by the river until moonrise, and even later, but instead I'll go split some green rounds, just for something to do. I'll have to be careful, though, not to miss the stump again. No doubt I'll still think of Gwen lying there, and of me holding her small, weak hands in my stronger ones. That's all I could do. There were no tree roots to catch hold of. Her life had gone on to surgery and radiation and chemotherapy, things I know nothing about—nothing like boats and currents and how to fish the steelhead that run in the fall.

Only Water

. . .

Good God, R.J.! Look at the size of that wave.
It gets like that. When the river's high. A mountain
of water.

A really *big* mountain—higher than K2. Holy bejesus.
More like a planet.

Looks like they're letting monster flows out at the dam.

So where are we supposed to run? The whole river
pours through that wave.

Start center, pull right. The only way to go.

What? Hang it out in the middle? Where that wave's
ready to eat you?

Start in the middle and pull right. After you pass all the
stuff at the top.

You can't get left?

That's a truly boat-sucking eddy over there, by the wall.

Looks like it'd funnel you down to China. And that
wall, my God. You ever been anywhere near it?

Once. I just squeaked left of the wave. On purpose.

Far left?

Well, it was really low water—not like this.

This is unbelievably high.

Yeah, Mare. Un-fucking-believably. Way higher than it's supposed to get anymore.

But it's only water.

Right. It can only kill you.

Gracias for the reminder.

De nada. And watch out for all that wood. Swirling in the eddy.

Looks like old logs, big as boat pontoons. I thought wood that big doesn't get down here anymore.

It doesn't. Can't get past the dam. Those must be from above the high-water line.

What, R.J.—from up on the slopes?

Has to be. From up here, in the talus.

So how high *is* the water, do you think?

Well, hell. It was fifty-eight thousand and rising this morning. Has to be over sixty thousand to float that wood.

Sheez-us. And we thought twenty thousand was high.

And now it's three times higher. Look there, Mare, the willows are washing away, going on down the river. And look—the old path is covered. We can't walk the people around on it. They'll have to take the high road.

Maybe I'll take it with them.

I'm telling you. Just do that middle-to-right run. There's nowhere else to go.

You can't cheat through that channel farther right, float over the bar?

Mare. No possible way. I've been there. It's floor-rip city.

I'd rather rip a floor than flip out in that wave. How tall is it, R.J.? Forty, fifty feet?

At least. I've only seen it taller one time. In the early eighties high water. It flipped a thirty-three-foot motor rig end for end. Like a rubber ducky.

You saw it?

Yeah. The wave stood the rig up and surfed it. The water looked twice as tall as the boat—like seventy feet. The boat fell back on itself, everything crashed down— frames, boxes, spare motor—right on top of the people.

What? That never happens.

And the scariest thing was hearing it, Mare. *Ka-whomp!* Like a tall building hitting the ground.

What'd you do?

What *could* we do? We radioed out for help and ran down with all the safety lines we had . . . hey, I probably shouldn't be talking about this right now.

Probably not. Go on.

There were floaters everywhere—people in the worst of it, people washed downstream. Some stranded on rocks down there. Just waiting to be saved, all along shore. Some had been trapped under the boat and were scared shitless. Took us a while to get everyone out.

Were they hurt?

Some. No drownings though. A miracle.

What about the boatman?

Quit that day. On the spot. He rode a Park chopper out and never worked another trip. I heard he moved to Phoenix and got a job in real estate.

God, R.J., can't say I blame him.

Hell, no. But it wasn't the worst thing I ever saw here.

What was? When?

Years ago. I was standing on this same rock, talking to an older fellow who called himself the Old Man of the River. That motor flip had just happened, and smaller boats had been going over. The river had dropped some, but it was still high and we wanted to quit our jobs every time we saw it.

And the wave?

Looked almost like it does right now. The Old Man was right here, and he was smiling.

What? God, R.J., if it was like today . . .

I know. I told him the wave had been eating boats. I told him experienced guides had been portaging their trips—rafts, coolers, kitchen boxes, everything.

What'd he say?

Not a word. He just smiled and showed no fear. He got out there in his little boat—it was a fifteen- or sixteen-footer—and sure enough couldn't make the pull. He got swept sideways to that wave and flipped.

No! He swam? Anyone with him?

No. Just him. He'd walked his one passenger. He washed through rest of it and on downstream—must've been in the river five miles before we pulled him out.

You pulled him out?

Me and a guy I worked with. We jumped in a raft and pushed out after him.

Did you catch him?

Only after he'd turned blue. He must've drowned in the first mile. But that's just a guess.

God, R.J.

God is right. Nothing like seeing the dead empty look of the Old Man of the River. After that and a bad flip of my own up in Oregon—well, it took me a while to want to come back. And I've never cared for high water since.

Like today.

Uh-huh. Just like today.

But you're here.

Uh-huh. Above Crystal again.

Where else would you go?

Like I said. There's nowhere else *to* go.

True Minds

• • •

Frank used to snore like a weed whacker, he told me, but had to lose the habit in Southeast Asia. The Navy trained it out of him, he said. Before serving in Vietnam, he used to wake up even himself with the racket. "I was obnoxious, Mare. Couldn't shut up to save my life. But now—negatory. If I can stay quiet, anyone can." He didn't say much else about his time overseas except that his patrol worked best between midnight and dawn. That's when they slipped into villages and huts to slit the enemy's throat.

"Three a.m.," he said. "Nobody can stay awake then. Not even the baddest-ass guys."

"God, Frank. What a nightmare."

"Yeah. It sucked. But it's not the hardest thing I've ever dealt with."

"What was?"

"Being home. Trying to be normal."

He kept to himself so much, I assumed he'd have no trouble staying quiet about our affair.

"You won't tell anyone, will you, Frank?"

"It's just between us."

It was a first for me, sleeping with another woman's man. On our river trips, I'd slip into Frank's tent after dinner and out before the moonrise. We were keeping us a secret—that and a piece of hidden treasure I'd discovered at River Mile Seven. I had found it while free-climbing alone on limestone, casting around on the wall, just playing. I was sort of heading for a cave about thirty feet off the ground. Pulling myself up the rock, I peered into the dusky hole. Something was in there, a basketball-sized object. As my eyes adjusted to the dark, a phantom form took shape.

It was an ancient water vessel. It had to be a thousand years old, left by the long-gone people whose dwellings and rock paintings were scattered throughout the river canyons.

"Mare! Dinner!" Frank called, from the beach near the rafts. His voice sounded small across the distance. Could he hear my heart pounding from that far away? Not much escaped him.

Resting my hands on the cool clay of the vessel, I tipped it toward me. Row upon coiled row of an early-style, corrugated surface looked familiar, but only from photographs. A crescent-moon crack broke the lip. Inside were a few shriveled spiders, wispy strands of cobweb, and a pinch of plant seeds. The vessel felt brittle and hard, more like metal than earth.

"Mare!" Frank called again.

I replaced my find and climbed to the ground. A soft sand path led back to camp. I vowed to tell no one—not the passengers, not the other crew members, and above all not Frank.

But after dark in his tent, his musky skin and soft kisses clouded my thinking.

"So what was up there?" he asked.

I got out of my clothes. "Up where?"

"In the cave."

He ran his hands over my naked belly. Fifty feet away, river current sighed on an eddy fence. As my mind went warm, I let slip my secret: the patterned clay skin, the tiny pack-rat treasures inside.

"I've always dreamed of finding a whole pot," I said. "Not just shards."

He stayed silent as I rubbed the hair on his chest.

"Ever see one?" I asked.

"Once."

"And you reported it, like a good river guide?"

"Hell no."

"Then what?"

"I hid it better." He yawned, my cue to go.

I unzipped his tent door. "Frank? You won't tell anyone?"

His breathing had already deepened. I leaned close to the tent and listened, but there was nothing to hear.

• • •

Days later, off the river, Frank found me at the boathouse repairing a worn raft tube. He informed me that his wife Emma wanted to meet me for lunch. As I listened to him, I pressed down a neoprene patch I'd just slapped over a layer of contact cement and abraded fabric.

I interrupted his stream-of-thought talk. "Did you tell her about us?"

His dark eyes smoldered. "She guessed."

"Christ." I leaned harder on the patch.

"Damn it, Mare, she's my wife! You've got to help me."

"Help you what?"

"Save my marriage."

"Unbelievable." I knocked the toluene jar too hard with my glue brush. Thinner soaked the newspapers on the floor. "Fine time to be thinking about that."

The stink of solvent filled the air. I stormed out of the boathouse, glancing back to see Frank dropped to his knees and cleaning up the spill.

• • •

Two days later, Emma called me, voice shaking. "I was a river guide, too, you know. Before I married Frank."

"No kidding. Where?"

"Here. Like you. But then I got pregnant with Crystal." She paused before continuing with words that sounded rehearsed. "I just think I should know you better. Frank thinks you're so special."

Not feeling very special, I agreed to meet her downtown. I drove to the Travelodge café as thunderheads above the La Sal Mountains creased the sky with lightning. A rain wind blew through my summer clothes.

Reaching the café at the same time as Emma, I almost ran into her on her way in. Her eyes poured out hurt—a lot like Frank's eyes, really. Her full head of auburn hair and smooth skin looked perfect, well cared for, not like my skinny, brown ponytail and nose peeling from sunburn. She was gorgeous. What the hell was wrong with Frank?

She chose our table, then unfolded her linen napkin and smoothed the tablecloth. She ordered white wine; I asked for water. As we studied the menus, she spoke without looking up.

"When he admitted he was seeing you, I wanted to leave him. It's too much to go through. Again." Hand trembling, she drank, then set down her glass. "But why should I leave? Really, why? I still love him. Our daughter loves him."

My appetite was gone. Still, my Monte Cristo sandwich arrived faster than expected—a mass of bread, ham, and powdered sugar. With the first huge chunk in my mouth, I was like the snakes we've seen on the river who swallow too much and get stuck digesting while everyone snaps their photos.

Emma poked at her chef's salad with fork thrusts that looked more and more savage. "You know, I'm mad at you. It's hard enough to keep a marriage going without someone coming along to sabotage it."

I nearly spit out a mouthful of half-masticated Monte Cristo. What had Frank told her? Obviously not that he'd made the first suggestion. Not that he'd tapped on the zipper of my tent after midnight near Brown Betty Rapids, wanting to "talk." Or that he'd shaken me from sound sleep at Dark Canyon to say how much a part of him I'd become.

Emma said, "But we'll be fine. We always are. I just wonder how you'll be." She leaned toward me—a bit— across the table.

I sprang out of my seat. Throwing down a twenty, I bolted out the café door. The thunderstorm had settled in, with veils of raindrops already washing dust from the sidewalk. Ducking under a store awning, I held my car key and trembled.

Go ahead and rain, stormy skies. You big talkers. You can't get into a certain limestone cave down by the river. You can't so much as move an ancient thread of cobweb in the shelter of the canyon.

. . .

That evening, my friend Jane joined me for a drink at the Poplar Place. "So he told his wife." She tapped a cigarette before lighting it.

"He said she guessed."

She snorted as a cocktail waitress brought us each a Sunrise. "And we have every reason to believe our precious Frank."

"Jane!"

"Well, hell, Mare. Aren't you angry?" She squinted over her cigarette smoke.

I drank, shuddering at the strong taste of tequila. "More like hurt."

"Huh." Jane pulled an ashtray toward her. "Why not quit him?"

"Frank doesn't exactly take no for an answer."

"Have you ever said 'no'?"

"No."

She arched an eyebrow. "So it's that good, sleeping with a highly trained murderer?"

"Jane . . . "

"Okay. But face it, Mare. He won't leave his wife and daughter."

Blood crept into my face. "Next subject, please."

She swept back her shoulder-length, ebony hair. "Well . . . my photography business is booming. I have a new show opening at the Main Street Gallery."

"Great!" I signaled the waitress for two more Sunrises. "To celebrate."

We toasted Jane's show while she sipped and I drained my drink. Then I leaned across the table. "Have you ever seen a Pueblo pot in the wild? Right where an ancient one left it?"

"Where?"

"I can't tell you. Only Frank and I know."

"Frank? Who lent you a raft to run your private trip? Who forwarded all your mail when you lived in Oregon?"

"You, Jane, but—"

"All Frank's done is cheat and lead you on."

"Thanks."

"Come on, you can tell me. Really, no one can keep a secret like old Jane."

Someone was feeding the jukebox again. The tequila filled me with vertigo. Still I began to sway when Tina Turner asked what love had to do with it.

Jane laughed. "Now there's a question."

"Jane." I stopped moving. "You promise?"

*   *   *

"Mare! Wake up! Listen to this!"

Heart pounding, I sat up. "Jesus, Frank. You scared hell out of me."

A bright sweep of stars lit the moonless sky. He knelt in the sand beside my sleeping bag, wearing a headlamp and holding a spiral-bound stenographer's notebook.

"Sorry," he said.

"What time is it?"

He checked his diver's watch. "Fourteen hundred. Two a.m."

I lay back down. "Aren't you an hour early?"

"Not funny. Mare, listen. This is us."

> Let me not to the marriage of true minds
> Admit impediments. Love is not love

Which alters when it alteration finds
Or bends with the remover to remove.

"I like that," I said. "'True minds.' What is it?"

"Shakespeare. Sonnet 116."

"Wow, he wrote that many?"

Frank's shoulders shook as he laughed, though he made no sound. Tearing the page from his notebook, he handed it to me with only the slightest rustle. "This is how our love is."

I propped up on an arm to see the page and his tiny scrawl.

"What about Emma?" I asked. "What about saving your marriage?"

"Oh. Yeah." He turned off his headlamp.

"Good night, Frank." I dropped back to my pad.

A moment passed. He sighed. "It's a beautiful night. In a few minutes the moon will come out."

I sat up again. Across the canyon, reflected light crept along the wall of rock—first a sliver of brightness, then a wedge, then an entire sheet of radiance. Down the beach, toads bleated like small sheep. The air smelled earthy from a breeze blowing up the muddy river.

Frank said, "That whole wall over there is going to light up like a pumpkin."

"You mean jack-o-lantern."

"Jack. Oh. Lantern." He put an arm around me, and we lay down together. Whispering, he stroked my hair as I drifted in and out of sleep. "We are true, you know . . . you and I . . ."

That night I dreamed about my hidden treasure. Moonlight didn't reach into the cave. Wind blew but didn't rock the vessel—it stood as motionless as any other bit of stone in the canyon walls. In the morning, my final thought on waking was of old, expert hands smoothing wet clay. Brown fingers pressed a bone shard again and again into the pot's pliable surface. The soft strains of a wooden flute mixed with laughter from the pueblo.

I opened my eyes. Sunrise hovered in a strip of light over the east wall. Frank was gone. He hadn't left even an impression in the sand beside me.

◆   ◆   ◆

As we floated past the cave on the next few trips, I scoped it with binoculars. Nothing seemed different or disturbed. Summer shifted toward fall—marked by muted light and cooler mornings. With the shorter days of mid September on us, I tried not to think of the coming winter. Back at the warehouse, I packed food for our last trip, humming as I filled the waterproof boxes.

Frank pulled up in his van as I was locking up for the evening. Keeping the motor running, he rolled down his window. "Mare, I have to talk to you."

"Where's Emma?"

"Back at the house with Crystal. Get in."

I climbed in and slid toward him across the seat.

He stared straight ahead. Driving south out of town, he followed back roads east of the highway. After some false turns and backtracking, we ended up on the road to the dump. We passed bulldozed mounds of old appliances, furniture, broken toys, and ripped sheets of plastic. Ravens rose up crying from the red dirt, and the sweet smell of decomposition filled the air.

Frank stopped the van near a heap of tumbled earth. My voice came out shaky. "Are you going to dust me? Throw my body in the dead dog hole?"

"Damn it, Mare." He whipped off his sunglasses. "The office knows."

"About us?"

"They're saying you won't have a job next year. Plus you've been dropped from next week's trip."

"Dropped? What about you?"

He looked at his hands.

"Frank? It's just me?"

He kept his eyes down. "It's the pot. It's missing."

"Missing?"

"Yes, missing! Or course, missing. You are so naïve. Everybody found out about it."

"How? It turned into a regular sideshow attraction and you didn't tell me?"

"Word got out. You didn't know?" He laughed, a short, angry sound.

"'Word got out'? That's it?"

He stared into the distance as late-summer raindrops sprinkled the windshield. "I do love you. That will never change."

"Shut up, Frank." Bolting from the van, I stumbled toward the nearest pile of earth. There were decomposing bags with unknown contents and the stink of death. My feet sank to the ankles in soft soil as I stopped short of some rotting animal. I screamed and scrambled to run, but Frank caught my T-shirt from behind. He reached an arm around me but didn't draw me close as he guided me like some invalid back to his van.

. . .

"Jane!" My mind swirled. Frank and I'd parted with few words, his claims of undying love cut off as I slammed the passenger door. "Jane!" I ran up the stairs to her studio.

Out of instinct, I reached into my pocket for a key but found only Frank's sonnet: "Let me not to the marriage of true minds . . . " I balled it up, jammed it back in my jeans pocket, and swung open Jane's unlocked door.

"Jane, you won't believe—"

Something on her desk stopped me. There among the catalogues, notebooks, and correspondence sat a dozen or so eight-by-ten, black-and-white photographs of a Pueblo pot. Stunned, I flipped through the images. They were all of a corrugated vessel with a crescent-moon crack. The object was arranged on black velvet, surrounded by shining, polished turquoise stones, and posed next to spiky foliage and broken rock near a river beach. I carried the photos with me as I burst into Jane's darkroom.

"Mare! Close that door!" She held a dripping print with metal tongs. "What wrong with you?"

"Oh, come on. You know."

She wiped her hands, and we both stepped out into the hall. Reaching for the photos, she said, "Easy! You'll wreck the finish."

"Fuck the fucking finish. You promised."

She opened the top drawer of her desk. Finding a pack of cigarettes, she pulled one out. "I just went to see it."

"But it's missing!"

Her dark eyes widened before she looked away.

"Who did you tell?" I asked.

"Me? I just caught a boat to the beach at Seven Mile, took some pictures, and hiked out."

"Who took you down the river? Frank?"

She shrugged. "We put it back."

"Where is it?"

Her eyes teared. She held the unlit cigarette between her first and second fingers, like she was flipping me off even as she trembled.

"You're to blame, Mare. Not me, not Frank, not Emma. You."

She turned, stuffed her cigarette in a mug on her desk, and rushed to the wooden staircase to the street. I ditched the photos on top of a filing cabinet and followed. After two blocks of trying to catch her, calling her name, I stopped.

The smell of early snow swept from the mountains. Jane's figure grew smaller as she kept going, not looking back. Plunging my hands into my jeans, I found the crumpled sonnet. Frank was no doubt at home now with his wife and kid, a fire in the woodstove. He'd be packing a few things for the next river trip before going to bed and lying in Emma's arms. Likely with no words between them.

A gust of cold wind snatched up the poem. I ran after it, whimpering as the wind carried the note out of reach. People hustled past, pretending not to see or hear, collars raised against the cold. The words disappeared up the street, and I ran after them—first sobbing, then cursing, then falling silent before I gave up the chase.

A Real Café

. . .

You may think someone's your opposite—neat where you're messy, tough where you're tender—until you run a river with him. Then as you're getting through rapids together, working long days, watching each other's backs in all kinds of drama, you get to see all the ways you're alike. Take Jack and me, for instance. When we first met, I found him as serious as sunstroke. He was all protocol on our raft-patrols of the winding canyons of the Yampa River and the deep, red gorges of the Green. Our jobs as backcountry rangers required we run week-long trips in silver army-surplus boats heavy with supplies: canned goods for the field stations, bags of powdered lime for the outhouses, picks and shovels for trail work— you name it. If an item was needed somewhere down-stream, we loaded it into one of our government-owned rafts named *Chub* and *Humpback* for the endangered Green River fish rarely seen anymore.

Jack and I had come to the job on different paths. He had been a ranger in various parks since college; I had been a whitewater guide working farther downstream. I didn't share the details of why I had switched to rangering—no doubt he'd find me unworthy enough without learning the sordid details of my previous life.

Our disparate dress vouched for our different backgrounds. My park uniform was likely the most crumpled set of gray-and-greens in all fifty states. Jack somehow managed to keep pressed creases in his sleeves and standard-issue slacks. Likewise my short hair stood up uncombed and wild, while his stayed groomed and in place beneath his mesh ballcap. I wore drugstore sunglasses from off the rack; he alternated between designer-frame prescription shades and spotless wire-rimmed readers. Well, I figured, never the twain shall meet.

One time when we stopped for a river lunch, Jack asked, "Pardon me, Mare. But do you know Laura? At headquarters? She works for Interpretation."

"Yeah." I'd met her. Laura spoke with a charming Georgia accent and moved with grace and liquidity. She gave polished presentations to the hordes of visitors who flooded the interpretive center, her manners smooth, her long, dark hair falling from her shoulders as she reached for the binders, pens, and papers that were her teaching aids.

Thinking of that flowing hair, I felt for my own and found mostly exposed neck.

"She wants to come on one of our trips," Jack said.

"Oh?" I spread a cracker with peanut butter.

"So? What do you think?"

"Well." I chewed my lunch. "She's cute, Jack. But can she dance?"

Because Jack could cut a rug. He loved to go to town on Friday nights after we'd reached the boat ramp at take-out, deflated and rolled the rafts, and driven back to headquarters. He danced as if he were born to it, his dips and spins infused with a rare grace. At the urging of any music, any time, he came alive—a dream in sneakers.

A few times, Jack danced with me. He didn't know I loved old disco films and had studied them to practice moves of my own. In his arms my funky improvisation fit his ballroom style like leotards. He twirled and tossed me away just to reel me in and toss me again. He lowered me until my spine brushed the floor, then he sprung me, weightless, back to his chest. Somehow our different approaches meshed, but, because Laura was watching, we seldom got the chance. Instead, during "Park Nights" in town, he preferred to sit beside her on a folding table near the wall, swinging his legs to the music—but not dancing.

One lunchtime off the river, we cruised in his green Ford truck to the Burger-Freeze for shakes and fries. The truck had no radio, so Jack kept an old tape player on the seat between us, snapping his fingers to vintage Sam Cooke tunes.

"Know this one, Mare?" he asked, as Sam sung about twistin' the night away.

I shook my head. "That's pre disco. Before my time."

We sat under the awning at the diner, Sam Cooke still with us and singing low. Tourists drove by on the interstate, heads swiveling to gawk at us and the retro diner. When the burgers arrived, Jack said, "Oh, by the way. Laura's coming on our patrol next week."

I sucked air into my chocolate shake. "Why?"

A blush crept into his cheeks. "To . . . learn about the park, of course. She can't get time off for the whole thing, so she's hiking in to meet us at Jones Hole."

"Fine."

He squinted at me through his glasses. "You don't like her."

"Like her? I love her. Come on, Jack, you're wrecking my lunch."

He punched a button that silenced the music, and we passed the rest of our break without speaking.

• • •

Near the end of our next river trip, Jack and I stopped at the Echo Park field station to resupply with drinking water. We always paused there before starting the six hot miles to the Jones Hole river campground. As we pulled into Echo, Jack filled the air with Woody Woodpecker laughs. His voice bounced off the opposite cliffs and through the vast space between the canyon's sandstone walls, filling the air with the reverberated calls of one high-pitched woodpecker, then two, then three. He giggled until his hazel eyes spilled tears. Reaching to wipe them, he caught sight of his watch.

"Uh-oh! Laura's probably at Jones by now. Let's skip the water."

"Not get water?" I waved him off. "You're nuts."

"Come on, Mare. We can fill up at Jones."

Gathering the empty water jugs, I started toward the station. "You go ahead. I'll catch up."

"You'll follow me?"

"Right."

"You'll follow me?"

"Yes!"

"Better not, Mare, I'll call the cops." He giggled again. "Just go."

He hesitated but only for a moment. As I settled the jugs near the station's hand-operated pump, I watched him row downstream as a cat watches birds out the window—curious, pretending to be detached. When I launched a half-hour later, I took my time, letting my oars dangle in the current, leaning back on my rowing seat. Thunderheads built to the west, growing like time-lapse flowers. At Stateline Rapids, I waved to the battered sign marking the edge of Colorado. Three bighorn sheep nibbled on penstemon in the north wall.

"Eat, drink, and be merry," I told them. "Tomorrow you may be in Utah. With *Laura*." The sheep gazed at me with goggle eyes before lowering their heads again.

At Jones Hole, I found Chub barely secured to an undersized piece of driftwood. "Great, Jack," I said to the empty beach. "Now I'm sure you've lost your mind."

Unpacking a safety line, I strung both boats to a sturdy Park Service stake farther from the river. Then I rummaged through provisions we'd brought for the Jones Hole ranger we called Dan-the-Man. I gathered all the food and supplies in my arms: spare batteries for Dan's radio pack, inflatable splints, new filters for his water purifier.

"Cookies, bananas, apples, and cheese," I sang to myself, as I loaded up. "Cookies, bananas, apples, and—jeez."

It was obvious there was too much to carry without using Dan's wheelbarrow. With a small bit of the fruit, I headed for his cabin, which sat a hundred yards off the main trail behind a stand of cottonwood and box elder.

Near Dan's place, the hypnotic rustle of green boughs stopped me. Mesmerized, I stared up at the rustling leaves, forgetting my task for a minute. Then I heard soft laughter coming from beyond the trees. I tiptoed nearer the cabin. Soon I made out the distinct sound of voices and the sight of Dan's big porch hammock swaying with the weight of two people. A woman laughed. In a voice dripping with Georgia sweetness, she said, "Picky, picky. Where do you get your notions, sugar?"

A man giggled. I knew Jack's laugh, and this wasn't his.

"What sleazes." I turned back to the main trail. "Sleazes."

Rounding a bend, I shouted the word again, then built to a full-steam run and nearly crashed into Jack.

"Whoa, Mare!" He laughed. "Who are you talking to?"

He was sweaty and covered with dust, his uniform shirttails as I'd never seen them—rumpled and hanging outside his shorts. He eyed the bananas in my arms.

"Why are you carrying those?" he asked.

"Just bringing a handful while I get Dan's wheelbarrow. Where'd you go?"

He removed his cap and brushed back his damp hair. "To the rock art at Ely Creek. Dan-the-Man said he'd had a report of some vandals up there. I ran up to have a look."

"See anything?"

"No. The rocks look fine."

"Figures."

Jack eyed me. "What's that mean?"

"Well, why didn't Dan go himself?"

"He said he'd be right behind me with the radio pack." Jack wiped his glasses. "Funny thing. I never did see him. Maybe we missed each other at the Ely Creek turnoff."

"Right."

Jack moved to pass me. "No big deal. I'll go get his wheelbarrow."

"No!" I shouted. A bunch of bananas fell to the ground.

He reached down for them. "Mare, what is wrong with you?"

"I can get the wheelbarrow. I have to . . . take him this fruit anyway."

"Okay." Jack handed me the bananas. "I'll go clean up at the river. Laura's supposed to be around here somewhere."

Back at Dan's, the hammock hung empty. I snuck closer to the cabin. Luckily there were no signs of life except for a few flies buzzing. Leaving the bananas on an orange-crate table on the porch, I found the wheelbarrow and aimed it toward the water. Down at the beach I stopped short when I saw Jack looking hangdog, standing by the boats.

"Jack?"

"I found Laura."

"Where?"

He waved toward the far end of the beach. "Down there. Wrapped around Dan-the-Man."

Parking the wheelbarrow next to Humpback, I waited while Jack stared at the water. After a minute, he said, "Huh. She never let on."

"That kind never does."

He looked up, his blue eyes dazed. Like he'd been slapped.

I climbed into my raft. Picking up two spare battery packs we'd brought for Dan, I tossed them into the wheelbarrow. Next I flung the case of water filters, then a Number Ten can of *Western Family* refried pinto beans. As supplies hit the steel with thuds and clanks, I hurled things harder. Jack watched open-mouthed as I lifted a flat of eggs over my head.

"Mare, wait! Don't break those!"

I lowered them. "You're right."

"Here." He took the flat, carried it to the wheelbarrow, and, just when I thought he would ease it down, he lifted it head high. "A pox on both your houses!"

He slammed the eggs onto the refried beans. The wheelbarrow fell over. Everything spilled.

"Wow, Jack." I admired the destruction. "It's a mess. Let's leave it for them."

We coiled the bowlines, pushed our rafts into the current, and rowed through Greasy Pliers Falls. We floated onto slower current as the sun set over multihued cliffs downstream. At a camp called The Cove, we cleaned up, cooked a pot of spaghetti, and drained two beers apiece.

Jack asked, "I wonder what Dan-the-Man thought when he found his stuff?"

"Undoubtedly the work of the same vandals who ruined the petroglyphs."

He giggled. "Bet he's mad as a wet hen."

I tapped my third beer against Jack's. "*Salud!*"

"God." His smile faded. "What does she see in him?"

"Oh, Jack, you're too good for her. You follow me."

"Yeah." He sounded unconvinced.

"You follow me?"

"Yeah!"

"Better not, Jack, I'll call the cops."

He was still laughing as he walked through the darkness toward his sleeping bag. I was left to listen to a flock of Canada Geese across the river and to stare at the crisp, full Milky Way.

• • •

The next day, Jack and I took off of the river at lunchtime and bolted for headquarters. We drove south on the highway, continued east past the Burger-Freeze, and stopped under a canopy of cottonwoods shading a real café—an indoor restaurant with two-page menus, bottomless mugs of coffee, and leatherette booths. We parked among the pick-up trucks lined up outside like horses at a saloon. Inside, we ordered chicken-salad sandwiches and orange sodas, avoiding the weary eyes of the other customers, men from nearby ranches or the oilfields south of town. They sat without speaking, appraising us in our sweat-stained park uniforms and silty tennis shoes.

A jukebox stood silent in the corner.

"You know," whispered Jack, pointing with his thumb. "It's still three-for-a-buck here."

I pulled some coins from my pocket. "Will you dance?"

Looking around the room, he raised an eyebrow.

"Okay, okay," I said.

At the jukebox I chose a few songs I knew, then scanned the labels for one more tune. I punched a third button, the only one with a handwritten name: "Beautiful Body, Bellamy Brothers."

When the music started, I raised my soda glass. "This one's for Jack."

We both listened. His blush began before the Bellamies even finished the first verse. My face warmed, too, as the play on words hit me. "If I Said You Had a Beautiful Body, Would You Hold It Against Me?"

My red cheeks had nothing on Jack's. He turned nearly purple as he checked the room for gawkers then stared at his plate. There was nothing for me to do, either, but keep my eyes down until the song ended.

. . .

That evening at dusk, as I hung my laundry from the trip, distant Sam Cooke tunes drifted through the housing compound. Overhead, bats fluttered after insects in the fading light. Then I saw Jack, his wet hair combed back, crossing the parched lawn outside his apartment.

He saw me, too, and stopped. I pinned up a T-shirt. He opened the door to his truck. I hung and smoothed a pair of wet jeans. He spread his arms wide, showing off his fresh cotton shirt. He waltzed, hand to his belly, in that style that I knew fit mine so well.

When he mouthed, with obvious exaggeration, "You follow me?" I nodded, waiting.

Then he dropped his arms, laughing like Woody Woodpecker—once, twice, three times—before stepping into his green pickup and slamming the heavy door. He drove slowly on the Park Service road, the sound of gravel crunchy under his tires as he cruised closer, watching me. Pulling past, eyes forward, he accelerated out onto asphalt. His truck hummed and his taillights burned red and receded beyond the sage and rabbitbrush. He was headed toward the music and dance floors of town, far past the bend in the road where the river sweeps south.

Sandstone

. . .

The paleontologist taught Erv that bones in a river settle parallel to the current. Erv hadn't figured that out,
though he'd worked at the quarry for twenty years before
the paleontologist arrived, green as corn, from Yale. It
took Erv some time to get over his first impressions of
the man. For good reason. For one, Dr. Case *ran* from the
housing area to the river every day—rain, snow, or summer heat. This was years before joggers were as common
as beehive license plates in Utah. Evenings as Erv headed
back to town, he passed Dr. Case running along the
quarry road in shorts, sleeveless T-shirt, and tennis shoes.
Dr. Case called running his meditation.

"You mean medication," Erv said, thinking of the pills
Betty took to relax when she was his wife.

"No, Erv. Medi*ta*tion."

It was the first time Erv heard that word used outside
of church.

Another reason: the paleontologist socialized with the
river rangers when they weren't on patrol, having them

to dinner, going on outings. Those two, Jack and Mare, laughed like jackalopes in heat, as if they'd caught the giggling disease while boating the Green River. Erv found Dr. Case's interest in recreation beneath a man with a doctorate in science. He scratched his graying head over that one.

Until Dr. Case showed Erv that the rock he'd been digging was old river deposits and the bones lined up the way the current left them, Erv didn't see the connection between ancient streams and the modern rock. He had noticed plenty about the bones he'd been finding at the quarry all these years, though. For one, he knew they showed up in little piles—or big piles, seeing that they were dinosaur bones. For another, most of the long bones—femurs, tibias, fibulas—lined up west to east. Erv knew it all meant something, but his job was just to dig.

He'd been hired at the quarry and had worked there forever, in spite of not having a high-school diploma or formal training. He knew his way around a rock bar and sledge and how to use the fine tools, too. And he could handle a jackhammer at any angle, which came in handy for the big finds. No wonder he was good—he'd started in the gilsonite mines when he was sixteen. His dad had left home, and though he wasn't ready, Erv had dropped out of high school to work full time. When he got the quarry job years later, he learned to detail the bones right where they lay, with ice picks and soft-bristle brushes. That was the meanest work, the hunching over with tiny tools for hours at a time. It just about did in his back and legs. Still, he outlasted the whole string of supervisors who ran the quarry for years before the paleontologist came along.

Sometimes when Dr. Case was running, his young wife, who'd also gone to college, followed along pushing their infant daughter in a stroller. They were out there even when afternoon winds blew up the river and kicked up dust and little bits of rock. Couldn't have been too good for the baby, and Erv wasn't sure what the wife got out of it.

One thing that rankled him, because he grew up Latter-Day Saints, was that Dr. Case used to invite in the missionaries just to argue with them. He'd studied the Book of Mormon enough to figure he'd found the loopholes, then he asked those kids into his home and debated their faith. He teased about Jehovah, who he called the God of the quick and the dead, and he got a big kick out of the Land of Moron and the angel Moroni, who led Joseph Smith to the golden tablets. Those things didn't seem funny to Erv, and he sure never questioned them. But he resolved that a man of science can't be called on to trust in the church or mysteries of the spirit.

At work, Dr. Case got to watching Erv and naming everything. Erv would clean off what he knew to be a shoulder bone, while Dr. Case put on his goggles and said, "Look, Erv, *Apatosaurus* scapula." Or Erv would finish with a string of tiny neckbones that Dr. Case called "cervical vertebrae from a juvenile *Stegosaurus*." Erv liked hearing the fancy names, and he surprised himself by remembering them. Sometimes, though, Dr. Case would hover, saying Erv should use a smaller-sized pick, or a bigger one if he thought the work could go faster, or that it was time to clear away the debris.

Then, one day, Dr. Case said, "Careful, Erv, you'll gouge the socket."

"I know it, sir. I'm being careful."

"Shouldn't you be using the number six pick?"

"Believe me, Dr. Case, I've done over a hundred ribs this way."

"Maybe so. But let's get this one right."

That did it. Erv peeled off his hardhat and safety glasses. He dropped the pick, walked past the office, and continued out into the parking lot. Dr. Case followed him all the way, asking where he was going, what he was doing. Erv didn't answer.

Dr. Case dogged him to his truck. "Erv, stop! I didn't mean it. You know me—I'm a paleontologist. I can be boneheaded."

Erv leaned against the bed of his truck and pulled out his smokes.

"I shouldn't have interfered," said Dr. Case. "You're the expert. I need you on that cliff."

That stopped Erv. He suspected deep down that Dr. Case would do fine if he chose to quit, which he didn't, because he hated like hell to look for work. But the man was getting on his nerves on the rock. Erv lit a cigarette and turned to him.

Dr. Case's dark hair blew in the afternoon wind. Behind him, Split Mountain stood out in the sun, bright and clean. His eyes looked that deep blue color the river turns late in the afternoon.

"Dr. Case, we've got to get a few things straight. Number one, Jehovah is not the God of the quick and the dead. He's the Eternal *Judge* of both quick and dead."

"Oh, I've been teasing, I—"

"And we say Mor*un*, not Mor*on*."

"Fine, but—"

"And I hate to say this, Dr. Case, but what you don't know about detailing bones could fill your library in there."

Dr. Case stood a minute, squinting in the low-angle light. He stared at Erv, then down at his feet. Finally he held out his hand. "You're right, and I know it. No hard feelings?"

"No, sir, I guess not."

Erv took his hand and shook it.

. . .

After that, Dr. Case began to spend more time with Erv,
asking questions and telling him things. Erv reveled in
the novelty of the talk. He'd never been farther from the
valley than Salt Lake City and hadn't had schooling above
the eleventh grade when he'd quit to help support his
mother, but Erv knew when he found something special.
He was the first to point out the almost-intact skeleton
of the baby *Stegosaurus* and the crocodile scute nestled
behind the *Camarasaurus* toebone. He called the paleontologist's attention to those finds, and Dr. Case put the
names to them.

One day as Erv was enjoying a smoke on the cliff, taking a break from handling the jackhammer, Dr. Case sat
nearby and dug in the broken rock.

"Look at this, Erv," he said. "All sandstone, but all different. Layers on layers of sandstone."

"That's so?"

Dr. Case nodded. "An old river bed. Millions of years of
sandbars building and shifting and changing."

Erv pondered that. "But these dinosaurs didn't live in
rivers. Where'd the bones come from?" All these years
he'd figured the quarry was a swampy place where the big
lizards dragged themselves to die, like the elephant graveyard in *Tarzan*. Dr. Case's river theory blasted that idea.

"Carried down from upstream. The *Dinosauria* probably lived and died throughout the basin, and the river in
flood picked up their bones and carried them here."

Erv thought a minute. "But bones don't float, Dr. Case."

"No, but they do roll on the bottom. Or they float if they're still in a carcass. And these were likely carcasses shunted into eddies by side components of the main current. Picture it, Erv." He reached out his arms to take in the entire cliff. "A river of floating dinosaurs."

"Ah," Erv said. "I can picture it all right. You mean bloating dinosaurs. You wait until spring—you'll see enough puffed-up cows in the Green to scare you off steaks."

That night after work, Erv walked to the public library to read about rocks. He couldn't get over Dr. Case's new notions, even though he'd been digging on the cliff for two decades. He found three good geology books that he spread on a wooden table near the magazine racks. He read about sandstone, that it forms in rivers and oceans and desert dunes. The rock can be full of calcium or quartz, tough or crumbled, gray or buff. In his digging, he'd felt the changes in hardness, and those were just in river rock. He couldn't imagine how ocean beach or desert sandstone would feel.

On his way out of the library at closing time, full of thoughts of rocks and rivers, he walked smack into his ex-wife near the Latest Arrival shelves.

"Why, Ervin," Betty said, hugging a hardbound book close to her chest. "What are you doing here? I thought you'd given up books."

"True. But I'm doing a little research."

Her eyebrows lifted, and her mouth formed an O. Erv saw she was tan and lovely, just the right amount of plumpness in her pink summer dress. Her hair looked grayer but wasn't permed as tight as before. It curled soft and easy around her face.

"You look great," he said, in spite of knowing he shouldn't.

She blushed.

He walked her back to the house, where he'd lived with her for almost twelve years. At the edge of the valley, piles of black-bottomed clouds and short curtains of rain hung over the mountains. The scent of sage blew in from the desert outside of town. He heard soft whinnies from the Searles' horses beyond the high school basketball field and sharp zaps from electric bug killers in the Rasmussens' garden. As he and Betty passed under the quiet rustling of elms, he told her about Dr. Case and how the quarry was once a riverbed.

"There's sandstone there where a river used to be, maybe even a big one like the Green."

She didn't answer, but she was giving it some thought.

At the house, the lawn looked green and trimmed. A single light shone in the downstairs window, where his reading chair once was. He wanted to open the door, walk inside, and sit and read as if time and disappointment had never pushed him from her.

Instead he said, "Goodnight, Betty."

He left her in the half-darkness, knowing she was beautiful and tender, but not knowing what to do about it.

• • •

In time, Dr. Case lost his pasty grad-school look. Maybe it was his meditation or just living in country with a wide, blue sky. He took up fishing. Every weekend he'd visit Flaming Gorge, or a mountain lake, or some part of the Green. He went after the fish whole hog, like he went after everything. In the quarry lunchroom, Erv found an article Dr. Case had clipped from the *Lavern Express* about Utah's famous, oversized German browns. Fishing catalogues covered the paleontologist's desk. Dr. Case bought hip waders, a canoe, one of those khaki vests with all the pockets, and a hat with a lambswool strip for keeping flies.

"I'm in heaven, Erv."

"No, Dr. Case, it's Utah."

He grinned, and Erv couldn't help but grin back.

Dr. Case was pulling in support for the quarry, too, calling professors and finding money for the digging. Erv realized that a man doesn't get all the way to a Ph.D. in paleontology without a burning interest, and Dr. Case was on fire. He'd travel to conferences in Laramie, Denver, or Las Vegas, or invite guests to the quarry for his talks that earned standing ovations. Every time, Dr. Case gave Erv plenty of credit: "the man who's learned his rocks from the ground up," he'd say, asking Erv to stand, or "the fellow who does all the real work." After a while, Erv got used to it, and he looked forward to going to talks at the quarry and swapping tales with visiting professors. Most of all, he looked forward to going to work.

One afternoon near quitting time, as Erv was using the jackhammer, Dr. Case waved him over. Erv shut down and took out his earplugs. The two men hunkered near a pile of ribs.

"Look, Erv, see that little tail of sediment trailing east? That means the river here flowed from the west."

"That seems likely."

Dr. Case pointed to a big femur heaped over with smaller bones. "And this legbone stopped everything else in this pile."

"How so? Like a traffic jam on Main?"

"Right. When one unit stops, it almost always concentrates the others. Or the bones are drawn into an eddy behind a rock. Not a lot of isolated pieces here, are there?"

"No, sir, I had noticed that."

"Well, it's no coincidence. It's physical law." He called the piles "waves," so named by a scientist at the University of California, Berkeley.

Erv climbed to an area of the cliff he'd been detailing. He pointed to two huge sauropod ribs stacked against an end-up vertebra. "Here's another wave, Dr. Case."

"And another," Dr. Case yelled from the top of the quarry, where two femurs, each about five feet long, leaned together easy and neat as dominoes.

"And this is the best one yet." Erv kneeled near a string of neckbones that curved around a nest of skull plates.

"Wait," said Dr. Case. "Don't move! I'm getting my camera." He climbed down the quarry face, trotted along a ledge of sandstone Erv had been digging in all week, and stepped off the rock edge where the light was dim. He tumbled fifteen feet down the steep path bordering the cliff's west end.

Erv scrambled to help, but the paleontologist was already sitting up tall, dusting himself off, by the time Erv reached him.

"No sweat," Dr. Case said. "Just a little problem with my eyes."

"Sir?"

"I don't understand it myself. Can't see much in the half-light."

"There's an eye doctor from Salt Lake who gets to town once a week, Dr. Case. You ought to go see her."

"I'll do that." He fetched his camera from the office.

The two men stayed at the quarry until well after midnight, logging the waves of bones and understanding for the first time what they meant. "This is it," said Dr. Case, his face weary but his blue eyes bright. "This is the beginning of something. Don't you agree?"

"I sure look at this rock a whole new way."

Dr. Case was quiet a moment. "Erv, I want you to come to Denver with me in September."

It took a minute for that to sink in. "Oh no, sir, I'm no professor. I've never even seen the outside of a conference hall."

"You know more about detailing than anyone I've ever met. You could contribute a lot to the meeting."

"Well, I'd love to, but—"

"Then it's settled. I'll authorize travel for us both." He checked his watch. "Holy smokes, I'm out of here. Tell you what—take tomorrow off. I'm going to. I feel like going fishing."

They agreed to that. Erv gathered up his things and walked outside. When he turned from his truck to admire the quarry lights against the Utah sky, he saw Dr. Case's office lights still on. Then they and all the big area lamps switched off. In the starlight, he saw Dr. Case lock the gate and cross the parking lot.

"Erv? You there?"

"Yes."

"It's a beautiful night, isn't it? I could almost believe there's a heaven up there."

"My heck, you mean you don't?"

"I don't think so—I haven't been able to reconcile religion with my work." He opened his jeep door. "What about you? You quit the church, do you believe in God?"

"Oh, yes, sir. I always have, especially in hard times. The church might've got on my nerves, but the Almighty never has."

"But what about the bones? You understand fossils. Aren't they an indication that life evolves? That earth wasn't made in six days?"

"Dr. Case, those are the details. I figure the Spirit is big enough to work them out. Or that evolution itself is His doing." The paleontologist was listening, so Erv continued. "To me what counts is prayers. I couldn't have gotten through any other way when my dad left and I had to quit school. Or when Betty and I split up."

There was a long pause. Finally Dr. Case said, "You're lucky, Erv," and waved good night. He drove down the hill—to his wife and baby and their three-bedroom home in the housing area.

Erv stood by his truck a minute. Cool air from Split Mountain washed down around him. Below the light burst of stars, he spotted a satellite on a north-south course. He remembered what Dr. Case had said about the conference and that he'd called him lucky.

"Thank you," Erv said to the heavens he knew were up above the darkness.

. . .

The phone call from Sheriff Hatch came twenty-eight hours later, when Erv was deep in sleep in his apartment. He had spent his day off in the library reading paleontology papers sent at his request from the University of Utah. Toward closing time, he'd looked up to see Betty standing by his reading table.

"Hello, Ervin. You're spending a lot of time here."

"More and more." He removed his reading glasses. "I'm preparing for a paleontology conference in the fall. Dr. Case invited me."

"My. Well, it's good to see you reading again."

He walked her home. They passed lawns and sprinklers and water-filled gutters. At the house, lilacs filled the air with sweetness. The same light brightened the window where his chair used to be.

"Betty," he said. "I'm feeling better."

"I know."

"I'm thinking maybe I can be somebody."

"But, Ervin. You always were somebody. I tried telling you that."

"Uh huh. Drove us both nuts telling me that."

She looked startled, then leaned back and laughed. "Not that you ever listened."

"Well, you know me—too thick to plow."

When he bent to kiss her head, her hair felt soft and smelled of the same lavender shampoo he remembered. Then it was all he could do to step down from the porch, with Betty half hidden behind her front door. But he wasn't ready, so he walked across town to his place. He sat up reading more of the dinosaur papers until midnight. When the sheriff called at five a.m., Erv was still catching sleep after two late nights in a row. He woke with a start.

"Erv? It's Jim Hatch. I need your help. There may have been an accident."

Hatch said he'd heard from Dr. Case's wife: the paleontologist had gone to Flaming Gorge and hadn't come home. She hadn't worried at first, because he sometimes stayed out fishing long past dusk, too excited to quit, and couldn't see well enough to drive until dawn. He always carried a sleeping bag in the jeep, just to be safe. But he had a CB radio, too, and never failed to call in. The wife was beside herself when she hadn't heard from him. She'd asked Hatch to contact Erv.

Rays of sunlight were just touching the mountains when Erv met Hatch and his search-and-rescue team downtown. The men stood in front of the station in their hunting colors, drinking steaming coffee from Styrofoam cups. They rode together in a van to Flaming Gorge, listening to the police radio, its static and garbled messages. Erv tried to calm his stomach. Hatch asked him some questions, which he answered as best he could.

"What kind of fishing does he do, Erv? His wife said he's got bad eyes—did he tell you that? He's new in the valley. How well do you know him?"

They parked near the dam, next to Dr. Case's white jeep. Hatch guessed as soon as he saw it that no one was inside—the windows weren't at all fogged. Erv wiped a bit of dew off the cold windshield. The mouthpiece of the CB was hooked in place on the dashboard. A sleeping bag sat on the front seat, rolled up in its blue cover. Hatch used a megaphone to call for Dr. Case, with no luck, while the sickening feeling in Erv's stomach grew.

Hatch headed to the reservoir while Erv led a few men downstream.

A band of fog hung on the river. The water smelled fresh and cool. The Green flowed fast and shallow, with narrow eddies. There were sudden deeper spots behind boulders that Dr. Case would have recognized as holes if the light were strong enough.

The first thing Erv found was Dr. Case's plastic lunch cooler, right by the river, with just an apple core and sandwich wrappers inside. Erv called again, and tried to run, but the boulders were wet and slippery. He had to walk instead, near shore with the other men who were calling for Dr. Case. Erv was hoping to spot him sitting up tall, brushing himself off.

He did find him. He knew where to look—Dr. Case had taught him. Sure enough, the paleontologist was in the river, his waders full of water. He'd washed into an eddy, where his arms trailed upstream parallel the current in the backwater. Erv pulled him to shore and turned him over. An eerie paleness had settled under his new tan. And his blue eyes—which Erv had figured missed nothing—were open, but the light was gone.

• • •

That afternoon he called Betty.

She said, "I heard."

They met at the library and sat out back at the picnic tables. The air was full of the sound of cars cruising Main and the smell of fresh-cut alfalfa from beyond the neighborhoods. Erv's stomach hurt the way it had since morning. He kept recalling those young eyes with nothing in them, a sight he wished he hadn't seen.

"He was it," Erv said. "He was the engine. I wasn't ready for him to leave."

Betty picked pieces of cottonwood fleece from the picnic table. "I'm sorry."

"And there'll be no conference now. No being somebody."

She didn't speak right away. When she did, her voice trembled. "I think you're wrong, Ervin. I think he'd want you to go to the conference."

"By myself?"

"Didn't he say . . . " She furrowed her forehead, thinking. "This is it?"

He swallowed. "'This is the beginning of something.'"

She nodded.

They sat for a time without talking. Erv was grateful for the silence, which she never used to allow. After a while she got up and smoothed her skirt. She asked if he'd like to come for coffee later on. Erv nodded. Then she walked home across the big lawn behind the library, arms swinging, flowered skirt swaying. Beyond her, light changed on the buff-colored cliffs of sandstone. Erv couldn't stop staring at them—would he ever? They stood this side of Flaming Gorge, with its legendary German browns and its cold, rushing stream below.

The Road to Bonanza

. . .

Antonia's first morning with the driller set the tone for the days that followed. They ate breakfast in separate cafés. They drove to the Green River in individual vehicles, Jet in the charcoal-gray flatbed with mounted drill rig and Antonia in her silver, four-wheel-drive pickup. They met out past the oilfield-supply warehouses at the edge of town, out the paved road that ended at a ward of the Latter-Day Saints, then beyond it on a narrow dirt track. Antonia arrived first. She slowed near the surveyor's stake that would be their first position of the day, parked, and prepared field notes in her heated truck cab while Jet backed the drilling rig into place. Then he, who'd sharpened his work teeth drilling bedrock for the failed Susitna Dam project in Alaska, stepped out into the ten-degree morning in full subzero field dress—overblown bunny boots, insulated coveralls, and black mesh *Torco Auger* cap under the hood of his fur-lined parka.

Antonia didn't join him until he'd penetrated the ground to five feet. Then she tucked her headful of

blonde curls under a hard hat with wool liner and
emerged into the crisp, startling air.

Jet began each hole the same way. He raised the drilling tower to vertical, an eager look on his face, until he'd
aimed the diamond-bit tip at a slender, eighteen-inch-
tall wooden stake. He fired up the diesel engine, which
growled and complained as if new to this, and held the
rig's round-handled lever in one gloved hand. Next he
drained the last of a cold soda, belched mightily, and
tossed the can into the nearest sagebrush.

"Fire in the hole!" he yelled, as he cranked the sharp bit
into soil. "Better get ready, geo. I'll have your first sample
up in no time." He lit the third or fourth of the day's many
cigarettes before turning his full attention to the changes
in density with depth and the rate at which the auger spun.

He and Antonia had been on different schedules since
before they met. Jet hadn't slept in two days before arriving in Utah: he'd flown nonstop from Anchorage, checked
in at the company's Salt Lake headquarters, and declined
to take a motel room there, saying, "Too many temples in
that town."

He'd opted instead to drive the flatbed east up aspen-
lined Parley's Canyon and continued south of the Uinta
Mountains to Lavern.

Antonia had preceded him there from Salt Lake,
through the snowy passes, eager to get started in her first
real job since graduate school. *This is it!* she told herself—
everything she'd worked for all her life. After spending
a day in site reconnaissance, she had checked in before
dinner to the Dine-A-Ville Motel in Lavern. She expected
the driller to do the same when he arrived that evening,
but he headed straight for the town's only private club,
the Cowboy Corral. He phoned Antonia hours later and
in slurred words claimed he would get back to his room

at the Dine-A-Ville when he was good and ready. She resolved to stay awake to meet him but fell asleep waiting up.

Rising at dawn, she'd been reassured by the sight of Jet's drill rig as big as a cement truck parked in the motel lot. On her way to breakfast, she noticed that pockets of snow had collected overnight around the rig's tall tower, lowered for driving. She peered into the cab and was brought up short at the sight of three massive books on the front seat: *Utah Mining History, 1857 to Present. Volumes I - III.* Reading the titles, she felt her heartbeat race.

Onsite by nine in spite of his night out, Jet worked like two men as he brought samples up through the auger. Without speaking he handed them to Antonia. She in turn clamped them to the chain vise on the rig's flatbed and split them open. Moist from first snows, the soil was still dry enough to crumble in her gloves. She wrote either "silty sand" or "sandy gravel" in her notebook, seeing a pattern in the layers: river deposits, thousands of years old. Ancient floodplain. Jet kept on through the subsurface, going deeper. Below the sand and gravel lay bedrock—hard as concrete and just as tough to pierce. When the auger struck it, Jet retrieved the drill tube, a dim-toothed smile on his face. Hitting rock near the surface meant it would bear pavement and they could stop.

"*Finito,* geo," Jet said, every time. "There's another damn job shot in the ass."

Working in the brightening morning, she told herself she could stand the driller in country as open as this. Utah was wild and stripped to the bone. Strange and beautiful—rock exposed everywhere, naked and honest. Scattered trees were the size of mere shrubs, casting scant shadows, nothing like the deep, oak-filled woods back home. Even the colors of the earth were different here: hills of orange, spires of red, stripes of yellow in bald topography that stretched to every horizon. She hummed Puccini, *La Boheme,* which had once been her father's favorite opera. In the sunlight, among many-hued rock and open-book landscape, she was far from the hidden seams of coal and gray tailings of her youth.

. . .

Back in Salt Lake she had asked her boss, "What's east of the Green River, Mr. Stevens?"

Dick Stevens hadn't looked up from his maps. He'd run one slender hand through his neat, black hair. "Badlands, Castanero. Empty desert."

Antonia studied the site plan, her hands on her hips. "So we're building a high-capacity road out there because . . . ?"

"Oh." Stevens squinted at her. "There's a ghost town out there. Called Bonanza. It was big on gilsonite extraction in the 1940s and 50s. Every old timer in the area worked in those mines."

"Mining town?" Her face flushed.

"Yes. Long dead." He unfolded a color brochure. "Look at this."

The photograph on the brochure's glossy cover showed a vast rubber raft on a muddy river. Seated behind a dozen smiling people, an aging boatman held a pair of oars as long and thick as lightpoles. The caption read, "Colorado River Adventures, Cataract Canyon, Utah."

Stevens said, "This is how we'll drill on the Green. We can load our rig right onto this outfit's biggest raft. They'll supply a veteran boatman to help."

He looked up, meeting Antonia's silent apprehension. The skin around his gray eyes creased as he smiled. "You know how to swim, Antonia? The geologist before you didn't. He gave his notice when he saw this."

Stevens laughed, a thin intake of breath. Blood warmed Antonia's face and hands. That they'd be working on water was news to her. Neither had she known about Bonanza and its mining roots.

She kept her voice calm. "I can swim."

.   .   .

Before noon on the third day of drilling, just after shooting in the ass their fifth hole of the morning, Antonia and Jet wavered in their work. They couldn't find the next surveyor's stake and so had to walk the ground, searching. Antonia came upon it about fifty feet off the road, hidden in a mature ring of sagebrush.

"Here it is."

Stepping into the brush to read the label on the stake, she felt her feet crunch something brittle. She jumped back as if she'd been bit.

"Bones!"

Jet came running. "Well, no shit."

He tramped into the middle of them. A jumbled pile reached to his boot-tops: femurs, vertebrae, ribs—crisscrossed and heaped together, bleached white, picked clean and dry.

He kicked aside a skull. "Coyote."

"All of them?"

"Looks like."

"What about those big skulls? Next to the three tiny ones right there."

"A whole family," Jet said, lighting a cigarette. He smiled and exhaled smoke. "Somebody did good work here. Killed the little bastards before they could grow up and multiply. Saves the government from having to do it. Shit, maybe it *was* the government—clearing the way for our road."

"But, out here? Why not just . . . "

He looked amused. "Spit it out, geo."

" . . . shoo them off." Her voice was small. "Let them escape."

Jet had already turned toward a rumbling out on Asphalt Ridge.

"Something's coming," he said. "Real slow."

"It sounds like a truck."

"Brilliant, geo. A big damn truck."

Antonia glared at him.

"Maybe it's the boatman." Jet checked his watch. "If so, he's right on time. Hell, I didn't know boatmen could read a clock."

A yellow truck twice the size of Jet's drill rig came into view. It had stake sides and an aluminum fishing boat turned belly-up atop its load. Grinding down the ridge, the driver was singing loud and out of tune to an old Willie Nelson song blasting from the cab's open window. He kept coming and slowed to a stop behind Antonia's silver truck. Turning off the radio and engine, he eased from the cab.

Antonia tried not to stare. Mr. Stevens' "veteran boatman" was the same oarsman pictured on the rafting brochure. He stood short and thick from top to bottom, with trimmed white muttonchops, Day-Glo orange hooded sweatshirt, and dirty, worn cap that read *CRA*.

"Greetings, earthlings." The grinning stranger shook Jet's hand, then bowed to Antonia. "Name's Bert. Are you the folks expecting a boat?"

• • •

That afternoon they labored until dark to rig the thirty-three-foot pontoon raft. Antonia, acting as crew chief for the job, used her truck's mobile phone to call in a crane from town for the heavy lifting. They pulled two gigantic rubber tubes off Bert's truck and inflated them, the air going in inch by inch, like blowing up an enormous balloon. They dragged each tube into place to form a sort of catamaran. Over the top of the rubber they slid a metal frame and tugged it into position. Through it all they spoke fewer than a hundred words.

After the crane operator left, as Jet worked solo tightening down bolts on the now-floating drill rig, Antonia showed Bert the pile of coyote bones. He pulled a shovel from his truck without speaking and got to work burying them. He didn't comment until he'd finished, and then it was brief: "Assholes used poison—or traps."

That night Antonia phoned in an update to Dick Stevens. She caught him at home, the sound of soft music in the background. "We got the raft rigged, Mr. Stevens. We'll start drilling the river holes in the morning."

"Excellent, Castanero. How's it look?"

"It might work. If the Green doesn't rise."

"It won't. There shouldn't be snowmelt until spring."

Antonia held her tongue. She'd learned from her father about ice, rivers, and mid-winter warm spells. But there wasn't time for that story.

Stevens asked, "What's your take on the boatman?"

"A good guy and a hard worker."

"Great. Let him know he can stay on as a drilling assistant. How is it out there?"

Antonia didn't mention her growing dread of the river job. Ice lay in the shadow of the streambanks. Soon more ice would be coming in sheets: she'd heard that in winter the river filled with floes you could just about walk on.

More and more the scene resembled the Susquehanna River, with its winter freeze-ups and fickle nature. She said nothing about her fears and nothing about the temperatures that were, in one of the driller's choice phrases, "butt-ass cold."

To Stevens, she said only, "There's excellent rock exposure. Everything's above ground—or close to it. Not much need for digging or stripping to see what's going on."

"Yes, except—" He stopped. "Never mind. Good luck tomorrow."

· · ·

Riding with Bert in the aluminum fishing boat each morning eased Antonia's dread of the river. He plied the many currents between land and the rig with obvious skill, even as rafts of ice sped toward them on the water's surface. The floes coursed all around, and he didn't waver. He just dodged them as if born knowing their ways, and he talked about the river with respect.

"She's feeling cold this morning," he would say. "Got to be extra specially nice to her today."

"Papa used to talk like that," she said, "about the coal mine in Port Griffith."

To which Bert would nod, his eyes on the route ahead.

Jet pushed himself hard, all the while smoking, bossing Bert, and tossing profanity like stones. One morning he cracked a drill bit trying to pierce a boulder—"harder than shit, but way too shallow to be bedrock"—and drove off in a huff to buy a replacement. Bert and Antonia waited for him on the rig. She wasn't convinced Jet would get past the Cowboy Corral and be back before dark, but she didn't say so.

Without the drilling jarring the raft, it settled down on the river and relaxed in its tethers from both shores. She sat cross-legged on the deck attending to her notes. Bert leaned against the engine housing, quiet for a long time.

Then he asked, "What got a girl like you interested in rocks?"

She looked up. "What do you mean, 'a girl like me'?"

He raised his hands. "No offense. I just don't know any scientists, much less female ones."

Bert's cap now bore a piece of duct tape that Jet had stuck on it, a felt-penned letter "p" inserted after the "A." The boatman wore the newly dubbed "CRAp" hat with ease—he must have known it had been altered but seemed to care less.

Antonia smiled. "Geology is in my blood. My family's been in mining since the 1920s."

"No kidding? You ever work for the coal companies south of here?"

"I could never have anything to do with coal."

"Right." Bert nodded. A moment passed before he asked, "Why not?"

"I promised my father I wouldn't."

Antonia started her tale at the beginning. Her Grand-papa Castanero had grown up in the foothills of the Apennines. He'd begun in the coal mines at age thirteen, more than a decade before immigrating to Port Griffith, Pennsylvania, during the time of Mussolini. Antonia's father and three uncles had also dug coal since they were teenagers. They'd worked the River Slope Mine in Port Griffith long before Antonia was born. When she emerged from the womb in that coal-slag town, it was with a curiosity already roused by the rocks. She grew up blackening her hands and clothes every day with the specimens she tossed and kicked apart.

Her mother would fret over her soiled jeans and coat. "Look at Tonia. Always filthy. It doesn't wash out, and she won't stay out of the tailings."

Antonia's father, Francesco, would only shrug, as he did at most things. "Let her be, Flo. She's got a brain, that Tonia. It'll get her out of this one-job town." Then he would shamble away to resume work on a crossword puzzle he would only half fill.

Years before, Francesco had never been without Musetta's waltz from *La Boheme*. He'd hummed it every morning: when he rose, when he shaved, when he left the house to meet his three brothers on their way to the River Slope Mine. Puccini's aria lived inside him.

Antonia told Bert, "I'm named after my Uncle Tony. He put money away for years to travel back to Italy, but instead his life savings sent me to college."

"Life savings? So he's passed on?"

"Yes. Same with Uncle Joe and Uncle Augie. I never knew them." She went back to her notes.

"All three? I'm sorry."

Many moments passed, filled only with the gossip of the river, until Bert whispered, "Antonia, look!"

He pointed to the east bank. She raised her binoculars. Peering across glistening water the color of green olives, she searched shore. First she saw just bare streambank and leafless cottonwoods until she locked onto an animal sneaking a drink.

"Coyote." Antonia scanned the creature's sun-tipped fur and tail.

"Dang. He'd better be careful. He's like Bambi at an NRA meeting out here."

"Worse. There's nowhere to hide."

She recalled the bones Bert had buried, the many sizes of skulls. Families, killed together—maybe even poisoned underground. And that bastard Jet, saying it was a good thing.

As if on cue, the driller drove into view over Asphalt Ridge.

Antonia let her binoculars fall on the strap around her neck. "Scram!" she shouted.

The coyote flashed a wide, golden-eyed look at the drill rig as if stunned it should speak.

"Get out of here!" She waved her arms until the animal wheeled to a trot downstream.

•   •   •

River work took a week. On land, drilling eight holes would have been a one-day job. On water, wet sands from the streambed flowed up into the auger and jammed the bit before Jet hit bedrock. Then he had to start the hole fresh, which he loathed and met with creative cursing.

"Damn this wet work," he said. "Flowing sands—always a bitch kitty. It'll take a buttload of hours to finish the eighth hole."

As Jet stormed and stomped, he jolted the raft and rattled Antonia, though she did her best to ignore him. She focused on her notes and sketches of the subsurface deduced from samples—beds of unconsolidated sandstone and silt, occasional boulders, massive layers of conglomerate. She had it better than Jet, whose drilling suit was coated with mud below the knees. Fine, green-brown droplets had dried on his face and hair. When he'd had to work without gloves, he'd pitted his knuckles with wounds. His skin had gone grayer with the cold. Still, he persisted in deepening the eighth hole until they hit a solid layer.

"That's it," he said. He adjusted the machine's lever to pull up the auger one last time.

Bert prompted him. "Another dang job . . . ?"

Jet stayed grim and didn't bite.

Glancing at Antonia, Bert tried Jet again. "Time to clean up?"

When the driller finally spoke, he snarled his words. "Suit your damn selves, you two. I'm headed to town."

Bert said, "I'll go."

"Wait." Antonia glanced at the freezing river, the lines from shore. They could have the raft out of the water and safe from any river-level changes in an hour. "I put the crane on standby. I'm bringing him back to help us button things up."

She made the call. Jet scowled but began withdrawing auger sections, passing them to Bert to stack like logs. The crane driver arrived and jockeyed his machine into place to swing the drill rig back to Jet's flatbed. As soon as that happened, Antonia saw Jet relax. She helped Bert drag raft tubes onto land and deflate them. Everything came apart in a fraction of the time it had gone together. With all the gear loaded, they convoyed with the crane away from the site right at dusk.

Back in town she called Stevens from her room at the Dine-A-Ville.

"Nice work, Castanero," he said. "Ready for solid ground?"

"Yes, sir. We'll start across the river tomorrow. Jet and Bert have punched out for the day."

"Understand. By the way, have the driller call me at home. I've got good news."

Antonia felt a red flag fly up but said she would. They signed off.

Fifteen minutes later she joined Jet at the Cowboy Corral. He sucked down beer after beer at a table near the dance floor. Bert had never even settled, Jet told her, his voice raised over the booming jukebox and Eddie Rabbit singing about driving his life away. Jet pointed with a lit cigarette toward the parquet platform where the boatman, CRAp hat removed, led a jeans-clad, red-haired local woman among the other couples in a happy, floor-hogging Western swing.

Antonia felt relief take hold in her. She reached across the table for the pitcher near Jet.

"Mind if I share that?" she asked.

"Suit yourself."

He lifted his own beer and sucked it down. His hair straggled below his plaid collar as he drained his glass. Forcing out a massive belch, he leveled a look at her, telling her she was in for a grousing.

She raised a finger. "By the way. Mr. Stevens said to call you."

"Call him now?" Jet asked.

"He says it's good news."

She filled her glass as he went looking for a pay phone. When he returned only minutes later, he poured himself another glassful and scanned the room with glittering eyes.

"So Monday it's just you and me again," he said.

"Yeah. We'll miss Bert." The boatman would be driving the big yellow truck to Salt Lake in the morning.

"We won't need him east of the river." Jet's eyes narrowed. "Ever been over there?"

She shook her head. "Mr. Stevens said there's a ghost town called Bonanza."

"Ghost town?" He snorted and looked around again, at the pool tables, the bar lined with drinkers, the dancers wheeling on the raised parquet floor. "You ought to get out more, geo. That *ghost* town's going to boom bigger than southeast-fuckin'-Texas. Stevens and his rich buddies are going to bring in coal from Carbon County. They'll light up old Bonanza brighter than New York City."

"Coal?"

"Yup." Jet paused to suckle his beer. "Stevens sold me some shares in the Deseret Plant."

"What Deseret Plant?"

"Only the biggest-ass coal-burning thingie in two states! Out across the river. You didn't know?"

"No one told me."

"You got to be smart about these things." He tapped his forehead and leaned in. "Very hush-hush. It's all going to come back. Banks, whore houses, saloons, mini-malls—all because of coal."

Antonia wiped sweaty hands on her jeans.

He raised a finger. "We had to push for railroad right-of-ways first. You know, to move the coal. But Stevens just told me we're as clear as the pope's ass."

Antonia stared, a bad taste in her mouth.

"Hee hee hee. Sweet baby bastard Jesus—it'll be great!" He chuckled, then laughed gaily as tears gathered on his lashes.

Bert returned from dancing and nodded across the room at his swing partner. "She's a great dancer. Too bad her husband had to break in."

Jet hadn't stopped laughing. He shook with glee, snorted, and spread his arms toward the ceiling. "Fuckin' A!"

"Antonia?" Bert wiped his damp, untanned forehead with a bandanna. "What in the name of Jehovah is going on?"

. . .

Later that night, after the inebriated Jet had turned in, Antonia knocked at Bert's motel room. After a minute he opened the door a crack and peered sleepy eyed over the little gold safety chain. She asked him to come help her, "out by the river."

"But there's a storm brewing."

She shrugged.

He stood a moment, considering. "Okay. Give me five." He clicked the door shut.

On her way to warm up the silver pickup, Antonia stopped at Jet's drilling rig. Once again she peered in the window. There it was—the three-volume history of Utah mining. She gazed back at the row of doors at the Dine-A-Ville. Quiet as the Port Griffith graveyard. She tried the door handle on Jet's truck. Unlocked. Reaching inside, she picked up the books—one, two, three—closing the door behind her with a quiet click. As Bert emerged from his motel room, bundled in a coat and watch cap, she crammed the fat books behind her pickup's bench seat.

Minutes later, she was accelerating onto Interstate 40 headed east, feeling Bert's eyes on her.

"Let's hear it," he said.

She sighed. "When Mr. Stevens hired me, he said it was to 'consult on the paving of thirty-five miles of back road between Lavern and Bonanza.'"

"Isn't that what we've been doing?"

"He never said anything about coal."

"What about it?"

"The whole road's about it. According to Jet."

"And you've sworn off the stuff. But why?"

Without a glance, Antonia passed the turnoff they usually took to the river. What to say? She had never told anyone about her promise to her father.

"Antonia?"

She exhaled. "It was the River Slope Mine Disaster. In 1959. Back home in Pennsylvania. You ever hear about it?"

"Don't think so."

"See, the mine was near the Susquehanna River—you know, they found anthracite way down under the river floodplain. High-grade coal. They weren't supposed to dig beneath the river itself, but they did, past the safety stop line."

"Bad idea."

"The coal under there was too good to pass up."

Crossing a bridge far upstream of their raft-drilling site, she turned south. The truck headlights swept over acres of rabbitbrush and sage. Three strands of barbed wire edged the road.

"My uncles and my father always split up during their work, two and two. Just in case, they said, they'd be able to rescue each other. All four of them were young and strong. Boys, really, in their teens and early twenties. But Jesus. The river was rising—this was January—it went from like two to fifteen feet overnight. There were ice floes, followed by some freaky warm weather, and . . . "

Bert waited. "And?"

"The river flooded. It broke through to that undercut part of the mine. The braces were sound, they'd checked them that morning, but ice water poured in on them, with eighty-two men down there. Including Papa and my uncles."

Bert whistled, low and long.

"Tony and Joe were in the crew right under the river. Papa and Augie tried to find them but . . . the water was three feet high and rising. They had to run the other way. It must've been like pushing through ice slush. It rose about neck high before Papa got roped out."

"And—the others?"

Antonia shook her head.

"God."

"Yeah."

She recounted the rest of the story: Papa worked in some new vineyards in the area and didn't make music any more—no humming in the morning, no Puccini, nothing.

"And I studied rocks thanks to Uncle Tony's money—he was the oldest. He'd saved up a nest egg. Papa put it toward my bachelor's and master's in geology, Pennsylvania State University, magna cum laude, on the condition I would never work for the mines."

Continuing onto open range, she slowed to allow a flock of sheep to clear the road. The route split and curved into limbs of a maze. At each fork, Bert used the flashlight from her glovebox to consult a topographic map. He hemmed a bit each time, then pointed which way to go. When they arrived at a chainlink fence surrounding a sign bigger than Antonia's truck, she knew Jet had told the truth. Block letters printed in red and black on a white background read:

FUTURE SITE
BONANZA UNIT 1
Deseret Generation and Transmission

"Well, I'll be sheep-dipped," Bert said.

"Yeah." Antonia slowed nearly to a stop, taking in the insult of the sign in otherwise open, unspoiled country.

They continued west along good, paved road to Bonanza. In moonlight the few remaining buildings looked whitewashed and new. But they weren't new, Antonia mused, not yet. She found the end of the pavement and kept going on dirt road. When they reached the east side of the river, they stopped near shore. The water plodded by, unchanged by their recent labor on it. The moon now hid behind clouds as the first flakes of snow drifted through darkness. Antonia couldn't see across the river to where she knew they had left tire tracks while derigging the pontoon raft and hurrying to town.

The sites where Antonia and Jet would resume work led back toward Bonanza. Wooden stakes positioned fifty feet apart, like fenceposts with no wire between them, marked a new route.

"Now what?" Bert asked.

Antonia slid the gear knob to neutral, pocketed her gloves, and stepped out into the night. With an ache she had felt since the Cowboy Corral, she wandered through desert scrub. She came upon a stake and kicked it. When it didn't budge, she put on her gloves to yank it up. Snowfall had become steady—still crisp and flaky, like ash from a distant fire. She continued along the road, knocking down another stake, collecting it. Bert followed in the pickup.

Soon he pulled up beside her and rolled down the passenger-side window. "You'd better get in. The snow's getting thicker."

"I'm not done."

"It's going to be a big one. Keep us from getting out of here."

She nodded but kept walking. Wiping away tears, she came to a third stake at the top of a rise. She drew the rough-cut piece of wood from the ground and straightened up.

First light was still hours off. The road was long and silent. Chilled, she opened the door to the heated cab, tossed the soggy stakes in on the floor mat, and climbed up to the seat. Bert drove with Bob Wills singing low on the radio as they followed dirt roads back through the badlands. A thin cover of white hid the tracks of sheep they'd paused for earlier.

In the middle of the Interstate bridge, Antonia said, "Stop, Bert. I want out here."

"No. Too cold."

She opened the door while they were still moving. Freezing air rushed in as she unsnapped her seatbelt.

"Criminy, Antonia!" Bert brought the truck to a halt.

She stepped out to the waist-high bridge railing. Chunks of ice careened into sight on the river gliding far below. Bert set the footbrake, hustled to her side, and took her arm. With a jerk she pulled away.

He seized her shoulder. "Don't!"

She peered into his wide eyes. "I'm not."

He relaxed his grip, and she returned to the pickup. Reaching behind the bench seat, she pulled out the three mining volumes and felt their considerable weight.

His eyes narrowed. "Aren't those Jet's?"

She nodded. "He's been doing a little light reading. No, dark. Very dark."

Moving to the railing again, she felt Bert's strong hand back on her shoulder. She allowed it to stay as she flung each book like a discus, one two three. They splashed on the water in succession and slipped below the surface.

"That's it, Bert. Another damn job shot in the ass."

He nodded to the truck. "What about those three—you know."

It took her a moment to realize he meant the damp stakes on the cab floor. She retrieved them and returned to his side.

"One at a time now," he said. "Say their names."

She invoked her lost uncles as she meted out a wooden marker for each of them. The stakes fluttered like leaves through wind roiling the sky, then dropped to the water.

They swirled at first, separate and lost, until they settled together to proceed downstream.

Silent reverence. Then Antonia howled—wild and animal, startling Bert but only for a second until he joined in. Together they yipped and cried, faces turned to the heavens, voices piercing the night. When they ran out of air, they stopped. The high, chaotic song of coyotes reached them in reply.

"A pack!" Bert said. "Perfect."

She laughed, unbelieving at first, then full of joy, until tears came and streamed so fast there was no point wiping them away.

. . .

Bert drove them from there. The distance grew between Antonia's silver truck and the site of the biggest-ass coal-burning thingie in two states. Snow fell harder, blown at an angle by a north wind, urged into the wipers that Bert had set on high. Antonia knew the way back, though no trace showed of their earlier tire marks. There would be no trace of their new marks, either, by the end of the hour. She would not come out with Jet in the morning, she knew, or ever. If there was to be drilling at the stakes she had not pulled up from the Utah high desert, it would have to be without her.

They continued at a slow pace, talking low about the Colorado River many miles south: how deep into the earth it cut, how clear the sky was overhead. You should go there, he told her: you could be a geo-guide. It was safe on the river when you knew what to do. It sounded good to her. It sounded possible. In the glow of the headlights, Antonia saw the way before her grow more and more light.

Gravity

. . .

We arrive late and stand at the back of the crowd.
"Can you hear what they're saying?" I ask.

Mare shakes her head. "Not really. She said something
about contributing to his enlightenment."

"Uh oh."

Mare giggles, then sighs as two-year-old Sammy
squirms in her arms and fights his way to the ground. She
follows as he wanders a crooked course toward the house
and buffet tables. I'm left alone to watch the end of the
ceremony over the dozens of heads before me.

The bride and groom, friends of Mare but strangers to
me, stand with their backs to the American River canyon. Spring-green grass reaches nearly to their knees.
He wears a slate-gray tuxedo with creamy white bouton-
niere. She is big eyed in a long dress and wide-brimmed
straw hat, her white train draped over one arm.

The noontime breeze bends toward me, carrying the
distant scream of a red-tailed hawk. Mare has said this
place brings back memories of working on the river: days

guiding tourists through whitewater, camping on sun-warmed beaches, sleeping at the water's edge. The breeze bends again and bears the final words of the wedding: "You may kiss." The bride and groom share a long kiss as the river's rush rises from hundreds of feet below, filling a hush that precedes the inevitable wave of laughter from the guests. The groom raises a triumphant fist. His bride smiles, all radiance and indulgence, as she strolls arm in arm with him to the champagne table for their first toast.

Mare and Sammy return. "I remember repeating those same words," I say. "'I do' and 'I will.'"

"I know, Sue." Mare's face draws in sympathy.

"Maybe it will work for them."

"It may still work for you."

"No way I would take Tom back now."

"You never know. It's not over until the fat lady sings."

"Show me where she is. I'll gag her."

The crowd is not supposed to dig into the food until three o'clock, but guests are edging close to the *hors d'oeuvres*. After the first hand plucks up a California roll, it's all over, and a scramble begins for foam plates and plastic forks. It's a pot-luck wedding, but not everyone has brought a dish. There's a bit of a shortage. Polite panic builds. I weave my way in and manage to heap a plate with potato salad, mesquite-grilled salmon and halibut, French bread, and foil-wrapped squares of butter. With my fingertips I grab two forks and two bottles of lime sparkling water before settling with Mare and Sammy on the redwood deck.

We share the two plates as the groom and his best man link arms to dance on the lawn. The two men lip-sync to the Rolling Stones, who wail *in absentia* from stereo speakers perched in open windows above the deck. The best man's hair swings in a ponytail past his shoulder blades, brushing the back of his matching tuxedo. The guests chuckle and applaud.

"They do dance well together," says Mare.

"Amazing." I nod. "Do you think they rehearsed it?"

The first champagne cork flies over the lawn and into long grass as the music segues to a solo guitar arrangement of Tchaikovsky's "Sleeping Beauty Waltz." The happy couple clasp hands to begin their first dance, their faces tender, their eyes meeting.

"Now that looks rehearsed," says Mare.

"Yeah. Mine was, too."

Mare nods, her eyes soft, then turns to her son. "Hey, Sammy, you know this song—'Once Upon A Dream.'" They sing together, the boy eager and joyful, his mother bending to hold him. Moments later, Sammy focuses on my empty water bottle and the serious art of depositing pine needles in it.

"Oh, Mare, he's great."

She nods. "Most of the time."

"Tom didn't want kids."

Mare reaches an arm around me. "It's okay. You'll have a family, Sue. Even Jack took some convincing."

"It's too late."

"With Tom, maybe."

The wedding party dances on the lawn. Arms wave, champagne spills, tuxedo tails whip and fly. Ecstatic couples jump and sing to an upbeat rhythm and blues.

As the best man prances, eyes closed, a sheath-wrapped blonde partner joins him. Their hips meet, neat and narrow, as they bounce to the music. Dirty dancing. I watch their energetic display until I cannot breathe.

"Mare," I say, "I have to go."

"I'm sorry. This wasn't a good idea. Here, we'll walk you to your car.

Purple brodaiea and wild iris line the dirt road that descends from the wedding to the river. The road clings to steep hillside. A wire fence and faded posts provide the thinnest barrier between the shoulder and a precipitous reach of canyon. I could swerve toward the edge and pull three strands of barbed wire with me as I plummet over the cliff, airborne for just seconds before the first great bounce. Maybe the car would roll a half dozen times before falling, perhaps in flames, to the river. The sheriff's team would spend days recovering my charred remains, no longer recognizable even to my remorseful husband.

But I don't swerve. I take my time, attentive to the lupine and poppies and clusters of wild onion upslope. The road levels off near the river, where the forest's fragrance drifts in my open window. Live oak and digger pine arch the road. The sound of rapids grows louder.

Something's wrong. Crowds have gathered at the river's edge. I pull over.

Mid-stream in heavy whitewater, a rubber raft is plastered on a huge rock. Four wet boaters huddle on the big boulder, clinging to the deflated and sorry-looking raft. Clearly, their guide is not with them. On the far bank, a group of spectators point cameras, wave, and shout. Guides from other rafts have pulled to shore and now rush on paths through the willows to help. I leave my car on the dirt shoulder, as drawn as the others by the scene's gravity: novices stranded on a wrapped boat in a cold river.

A young, dark-haired guide stands poised on land, watching the foaming water. She must be the missing guide; she must have fallen out mid-run. She can't be much older than nineteen. Strapped to her lifejacket is a diving knife. Arms crossed, in all stillness and deliberation, she studies the currents. Then, with a great rush and

lift of arms, she plunges and swims, head down, angled
into the stream, to reach the rock.

"Right," I say.

Her arms churn, her legs kick. The eyes of the ship-
wrecked paddlers are on her, their shoulders sagging as
she washes downstream past them. As the river carries
her away, it seems there's no hope, but she keeps stroking, stroking, not giving up. Her determination drives her
forward and into the tail end of the eddy. She rides its
current into splashing surge against the rock.

"So now what?" I ask. "Now you're marooned, too."

She clambers up to talk with her people. They shake
their heads. She confers with them for many minutes
while none of them looks convinced. Nothing changes
until it does: she checks the straps on their lifejacket,
leads all five to the edge of the rock. Joining hands, they
jump into the current and pull apart, washed through
the tail waves to the bottom of the rapids. In moments
they have thrashed their separate ways to shore, where
the dark-haired guide herds them up a boulder bar, away
from danger.

"Of course," I say, convinced I never doubted her.

It's not until I have driven to the narrow river bridge
that the tears come. They cover my face, and I let them,
as I remember another dark-haired girl who tried and
never stopped, who didn't give up even when it seemed
there was no hope. My hair is shorter and laced with silver now, but I'm still the same girl.

Parking near the Coloma Grange Hall, I walk back
across the bridge. Mid-river, I lean over the downstream
wall, my weight against old stone. A few leaves course
on the water beneath me. They dip, rise, and are carried
downriver.

The Wish

• • •

B Barton has water deep in his bones, but you can't
tell it by looking. His face is leathered and creased,
and his arms are as tan as adobe up to the elbows where
he rolls his shirtsleeves. I look at B and think sun, dust,
and wind—desiccated before his time—and like me not
much over thirty. Never in a million years did I suppose
when he first came through the Oasis's double doors that
he's connected to things wet. He's got the best spring in a
hundred miles, and he knows groundwater the way most
people know their names. Why he looks drier than the
dirt roads leading here beats the hell out of me.

Maybe it's this place. Most of it's drier than lizard skin.
Canyons reach from town in all directions, no streams
in them—just rock and gravel, cleared out by heat and
wind. Here and there around the backcountry you find
wells and a couple of pretty green springs like the one B
lay claim to. Any water you stumble on is more precious
by far than the gemstones the average rockhound spends
years seeking in the mountains.

Or maybe we're drawn to opposites, which would explain B's being here, as well as the presence of the rest of the misfits who come in search of a suitable geography. Or, as B says, "Not misfits, Sue—iconoclasts." None of us could have picked a more arid place to land, just thirty miles east over the Amargosas from Badwater and Death Valley. Outside the Oasis, our main street is as dry as those godforsaken pieces of earth.

Definitely an iconoclast, that B. Not an easy one to know. At first I saw him in here only a few times a month. When he did turn up, the rest of the guys would pause at the bar and pool table like they'd been expecting him. They'd all listen long enough to hear his jeep grind to a stop out in the lot. Soon B would push open both front doors, flooding the room with daylight. He'd stretch his neck like it hurt and settle in front of me at the bar. The others would go back to their drinks and pool shots.

"Evening, B," I'd say.

"Good evening, Sue."

I'd set him up with three full glasses of water, no ice, followed by a mug of draft. He always hit the water first, lifting each glass in turn. When he brought the water to his lips, there was no gulping. No obvious chugging. He just slid the water in, as Fred the caretaker of the Herkimer Guest Ranch said, "like he was a quart low and about to burn the engine."

B's good looks throw you. He's got eyes so blue you'd think you were gazing through him to the sky. He has manners, too, which believe me out here is rare. When I took this job two years ago, he came in and asked in his polite way for the waters and beer. As I poured, he walked back out to his jeep and I thought, oh hell, he's gone, but he returned with a paper bag of crystals to show me—all amethyst, all sizes. He drew pictures on a handful of cocktail napkins: maps, arrows, scribbled words. He sketched wild canyons all around the desert where he'd found hidden gemstones. Standing across the bar from him, I lost my sense of east and west in deep, winding gorges. I could have drowned in his tales of palm oases below cliffs stark enough to be on the moon. All this beauty I'd never seen, edged with wind-rustling fronds of water-loving trees, all described by him.

One time B pulled out a small, perfect violet crystal. "This is my favorite. At first I thought it was just a big flake of mica."

It had been a gleam in the sand along the Amargosa River, a shine in the dust he'd passed up at first. He'd dug down and glimpsed more of it, then kept going, following the sparkle. When he lifted it out, he was holding a well-formed amethyst with color as deep as lilacs. No bigger than my thumb, that crystal. Its unpitted faces shined like the sky after a storm.

. . .

Months passed, and B took to spending more time at the Oasis. Often he promised he'd take me far up his canyon to see his spring. After too long of hearing that, I said, "You know, B, I'm starting to think you're full of it. All these beautiful places only you know about. This famous spring of yours where nobody goes."

He lifted his right eyebrow—a peeved look. "I'm going there tomorrow. I'll take you. We can meet here, right out front."

I told him I'd believe it when I saw him in the morning.

That evening I closed up the Oasis by myself. The last thing I did before going home was clean the bathroom in back. I washed the sink and mirror first, then the toilet

as fast as I could scrub it. As I mopped my way out of the
little room, I stopped to pull outdated announcements
off the wall. Of course I didn't touch the timeless bumper
stickers that would have been hell to peel off anyway,
things like "Women Want Me, Rocks Fear Me" and "I'm
Retired—I Was Tired Yesterday and I'm Tired Again
Today." Truly laugh riots.

There were business cards, too, thumb-tacked up by
everybody from farriers to haircutters. Then there was
the thing I always read last, a poem typed on a sheet of
yellowed paper that I would never remove.

The Wish

> Oh! To see blue waves
> Roll mute upon the shore
> Shells with all their secrets
> Sweep back into the foam
>
> Oh, if you and I
> Met as sea meets sky
> Suffused. Never ending
> Blending, damp with fog

Those few words captured the coast where I grew
up: the gray skies I didn't miss, the rain I did. I offered
my usual prayer to the page and asked it for a sign that I
should stay in the desert. Nothing came, so I sighed and
finished closing, as lonely as a fish in Death Valley.

In my trailer across the highway, I lay on my bunk
listening to jazz: Wes Montgomery, Bill Evans, and Thelo-
nious Monk on a CD mix I'd burned years before. Music
washed through me. As the tunes drifted low, they eased
me down; as they climbed high, they lifted me up. Soon I

felt as light as a cork on water, and sleep carried me away.

• • •

B arrived at the Oasis at first light. I'd dressed to go, just in case. We drove east toward Tecopa Pass, no words between us. Rays of sun brightened the sky but hadn't yet hit ground. B kept his jeep radio on but turned low, playing mostly the scratchy sound of static. The skinny dirt road, bent by the curve of the earth, went all the way to the horizon. There were few crossroads to speak of. Hawks sat on telephone poles, watching the ground. Over it all—road, poles, hawks, mountains—the morning light flowed soft. It wasn't harsh, or rough. B took it all in with the familiarity of someone moving through his backyard.

Once we crossed Tecopa Pass, we entered another dry valley, staying on the graded road. According to B, we were climbing into the Kingston Range. Passing the sign and turnoff to the Underdog Mine, B and I glanced up the wide canyon. Two hard-working family men had been at their jobs up there for twenty years: Barry and Jerry, the only miners who ever brought their wives when they visited the Oasis. Fred from the Herkimer had said more than once that Barry and Jerry were "the best of the friggin' lot." They got plenty of talc from the Underdog, more than came from any other mine in the Kingstons. As I thought of Fred, we passed the spur road to his guest ranch, marked only by a modest wooden arrow.

B drove on. After climbing a minute more, we pulled onto a track through scrub and scattered yucca. Back from the main road, B stopped at the mouth of his canyon to open a gate. We continued beyond the fence into a stand of willows and cottonwoods, not parking until we arrived at a tiny camp kitchen. My heart lifted when

I saw the sedge-lined pool beside his stove and roll-up table. Maidenhair fern grew at the fringes; dragonflies as big as hummingbirds darted over the unruffled surface. A mockingbird whistled, then chattered, then warbled. Clear, inviting water flowed from a pipe, and B stuck his hand into the stream. His eyes glowed as he wet his fingers.

"All this water comes from your spring?" I asked.

He nodded and motioned toward the mountain. "And there's more farther up. We can walk up there sometime when it's not so hot."

Another bird called from across the pool. Its voice started low, climbed high, and then fell again. B frowned.

"Quail," he said. "Hear that? Always singing my wife's name. 'Re-BEC-ca. Re-BEC-ca.'"

My heart dropped at the mention of a wife, but I said, "I'm married, too. My husband was a logger in Fort Bragg."

"Ah." B pulled a dandelion from the edge of the pool. "You lived on the ocean."

"Yeah. The opposite of here."

He studied me. "Rebecca was from Astoria, in Oregon."

Astoria and Fort Bragg had rain in common. Storms blew in off the sea, black and sudden. Tom and I used to hold each other in bed, listening to gales we thought would lift the roof. The wind and rain pinned us to the sheets, like ocean-going birds forced onto rocks along shore.

"Is Rebecca up there now?"

"No. She's been dead five years."

"I'm sorry."

He shook his head. "Where's your logger husband?"

"Las Vegas. At Harrah's, dealing blackjack. We're . . . separated."

Tom's logging job had ended when the big trees got scarce. He moved to Vegas a few months ahead of me. By the time I had sold our home in Fort Bragg to follow him, he'd been sharing his apartment with a stripper for three weeks. He couldn't resist all that skin, he said, after years of seeing women dressed only in wool plaid.

I shrugged. "I found the Oasis job in the penny paper and applied."

B sorted through a few stones on the dry earth between us. He picked up a gray one no bigger than a deck of cards. "Sue, do you know what this is?"

"A rock."

"What kind?"

"A gray one." I shrugged. "Marble?"

"No. It's much softer than that. Feel it, you can scratch it with your thumbnail." He put the smooth, flat rock in my hand.

My heart leapt at his touch. "It . . . feels greasy."

"It's talc. A clay mineral—with water in its structure. You've heard of it, right? Soapstone? Rocks don't come much softer." He leaned close and whispered. "Its name comes from the Arabic. *Talk*. Means it's full of secrets. It only shares them when . . . heated."

My blood pounded so hard I was sure he'd notice.

· · ·

That evening B stayed for dinner at my fold-down table. He washed dishes and I dried as we listened to Sonny Rollins on the CD player. I swayed to the rhythm of the saxophone. When we'd finished cleaning up, I made a pot of decaf. B and I sat down with His-and-Hers mugs that Tom had bought one morning from the Tradewinds coffee shop in Fort Bragg; when he'd left for Vegas, he'd left the "His" behind.

"Sue, what's this music?"

"Old standards. Jazz. I never get tired of it."

"Jazz has always left me cold."

"No way."

"What do you like about it?"

I shrugged. "I can't explain it."

"Try." He smiled the short distance across the table.

"Well. It takes its time, and I like that. There's the head—the melody—at the beginning. Followed by all the improvising. The players try on the song in every imaginable way. They just . . . take off with it."

B nodded. "Go on."

I closed my eyes. "It doesn't travel a straight line. The music wanders, but it doesn't get lost. It explores, you know? Then it returns to the head, sounding much—" I stopped, feeling self conscious about him watching.

"Much?"

"Deeper. When it comes back to the head, it enters my veins, is all I can say. It drives in more than if it hadn't strayed. Like—the rewards are greater for all that searching. The sweetness is sweeter, or shininess shinier, like . . . "

"Like?"

"Like a gemstone."

What I didn't say was, *like that perfect amethyst crystal you dug up on the Amargosa. After all those years of looking.* "And then I'm found. I'm back to where I started and at the same time farther along. I'm where I've been wanting—wishing—to be. And I feel lucky. Like I'm home."

I opened my eyes. A startled-looking B faced me. He got to his feet a bit at a time, stretching his neck like it pained him. *Oh, crap,* I thought, *he's leaving.* But no, he leaned across the table and kissed me. It was long and slow, turning over a warm feeling inside me.

Then he pulled back, his eyes wide like he'd forgotten something. "I'd better go." A moment later he pushed out the door of my trailer.

No, I yearned after him. *Don't go.*

. . .

B stayed clear of the Oasis for days after that. He didn't stop in once, not even to town as far as I knew, which after having kissed him put me in a state of mind. The other guys noticed, and they asked lame questions, like "Hey, Sue, where'd you hide the body?" and "Does this mean the wedding's off?" Real jerk-off material. When forty-eight hours passed and there was still no B, I called Fred to ask if he knew anything, if he'd seen B coming and going. He said no, but he would check around.

"He's hid out before," Fred said. "Since his wife died. But damn. It's been a while."

One night after work, I lay in the dark listening to Monk. B was on my mind even as the music played— through patterns of climbing scales and improv that went on like a long dream. The flow of notes stopped transporting me as I thought of B, so I turned on the light. My mind wouldn't settle. A few minutes later, I heard scratching on my screen door. I sat up.

"B?"

"No, Sue, it's Fred. Sorry. I never did know how to knock on these things."

"No problem, Fred. Come in." I pulled a fleece over my jammies and went to meet him.

"Can't stay. Been in Vegas and have to get back to the ranch." He stood outside with his hands in his overall pockets. "Has he showed?"

"No." I opened the door and stepped onto my wooden stairs.

"Figures. It's that damn spring of his. He's worked it like a slave since he lost Rebecca four—no, five—years ago."

"How'd she . . . pass on?"

He pushed back his cap. "It was the weirdest friggin' thing. She had that illness where you can't eat or drink—what's that called?" Fred looked away. "Oh, yeah. 'Failure to thrive.'"

"But only seniors and babies get that."

"No. Anybody can. She hated it here, couldn't stand things dry. Still, I mean, come on. No one thought she'd up and dehydrate herself to death. After that B worked around the clock to improve his spring. Planted new palms, rows of them. He told me, 'Where there are trees, there's water.' Damn. I always thought it was the other way around."

That figured. On the north coast, the creeks all but stopped flowing when the forests were cut. Once the logging robbed them of shade, entire watersheds went dry.

B transformed the Golden Rule claim. He built rock structures to deepen the pools. He added cottonwoods and willows to the palm groves to attract songbirds. He showed Fred how to restore the oasis at the Herkimer, too. "He helped me bring it back. Now I've got hummingbirds and dragonflies. Happy as larks. Bighorn sheep stop for shade under my ring of palms. I've got shrubs with little red berries the guests go ape for. Hell, you've seen the place."

"It's the best around."

"Nope." Fred shook his head. "That would be B's upper spring. The Herkimer's naked as a baby's butt compared to the Golden Rule. He's got so many birds you could be at the damn zoo. He's raised the water table back up. Like he's a friggin' magician—it's wet so near the surface it seeps into your bootprints when you walk the dry beds. B did all that."

"Not in time to save Rebecca."

He paused. "She wasn't too tough. Fragile, even. Kind of an Emily Dickinson type, into poetry. As if—well, you've seen her writing. In the bathroom at the Oasis? A poem called 'Hoping' or 'Wishing' or . . . "

"'The Wish'?"

"That's it. She wrote that. B put it up there."

*   *   *

After Fred left, I kept picturing B out at his spring, working late into the night. And keeping his upper spring to himself. It pissed me off, him staying away like that. The more I thought about it, the more mad I got, so I dressed for a drive and headed for the washboarded road toward his claim. There was no moon. Other than my headlight beams and the dust blowing up red in my taillights, everything looked dark—the blackness of sky and mountains blending together.

Light shone from the pass, in the direction of B's canyon and spring. Some of the ridges were lit up like the sun was still out. As I drove closer, I saw it wasn't B's claim shining like a million diamonds. It was the Underdog, Barry and Jerry's talc mine.

When I stopped and stepped out of my pickup, I heard the ringing of metal against metal, then silence for a minute, then the grinding of a power saw blade, followed by more metallic ringing. I couldn't see much, just an eerie glow cast onto the rock walls. The noise came and went, stopping now and then before starting up again with more fury.

After many minutes, I saw someone coming from up the road, first obvious only as a pair of khaki pants, then as a white shirt above them, growing bigger. It had to be B, lit up by the radiance from the canyon. When he came near, I saw his smile, his teeth gleaming bright in his tan face. I was about to ask where in hell he'd been all these days, but the cacophony started again at the talc mine so I had to yell.

"B, what in God's name is going on up here?"

"Beats me! It's like Dante's inferno!"

He pulled a small flashlight from his hip pocket but kept the beam off as he waved me to follow him across the road. We moved like two cats, B first and me behind him copying his stealth walk. As we passed the Underdog's base camp, I couldn't help but feel underwhelmed by the bare-bones outdoor kitchen with its canned food, dishes drying on a card table, and row of beat-up five-gallon jugs for their water supply.

During a break in the noise, I whispered, "*This* is 'the best of the lot'?"

"Shh. If they find us here they might get nasty."

"Right, B. Barry and Jerry nasty?"

"I'm serious. That emergency clinic in town is there for a reason. Plenty of miner's heads have been busted over places like this."

We pushed through the willows and rushes. Where the plants ended, we stopped at a dark, damp spot on the ground. B lit it with his flashlight.

"I thought so," he said.

"What?"

"They must've blasted the mother rock all to hell. Look at this sorry piece of guano. It used to be the twin sister to my oasis, but I'm guessing it drained out through fissures they made with their dynamite."

He sounded so sick about it, I wanted to reach out for his hand. Instead I could only follow him up the canyon as he took off again, now lighting our way through ocotillo and cholla. After I'd trailed him a minute, we edged together onto a rock ledge where we could look down on the Underdog. Out in the open a hundred feet below, Barry and Jerry wore goggles and hardhats and labored over a huge wooden workbench that looked as unmovable as bedrock. A generator ran klieg lights that flooded the place with eye-stunning brightness. Between the mighty hammer swings that crashed metal on metal, the tiny sound of their boombox broke through the din. I knew the music, though I no longer listened to that genre: Led Zeppelin, from the *Hindenburg* album.

We watched them sweat in the cool night air for just a few minutes before B signaled that we should leave. I followed him again, through the skeletal desert flora, then along the road to my truck. He leaned in, and I thought he'd kiss me, but he didn't. He turned to go.

"I know about Rebecca!" I shouted after him.

He wheeled back to me, his eyes flashing in the glow from the canyon.

I swallowed. "I just want to say it's okay."

"Okay?"

"Fred told me the desert killed your wife."

B's mouth fell open. "That's what people think?"

"I love 'The Wish.'"

He snorted. "It failed."

"What? To bring water? To . . . ?"

He shot me an angry look, and in a second he was gone. His white-shirted figure grew smaller and more dim, then went to nothing, as he jogged up the road to the Golden Rule.

Crap. There wasn't anything to do but retreat the other way, into the darkness I'd come through earlier.

When I reached my trailer, I put Monk on the CD player. I listened, wondering what to do. Call Fred to tell him B was all right—if you could call it that? No. Fred, like most normal people at two a.m., would be sound asleep.

·   ·   ·

Days later B knocked on my trailer door so early the sun hadn't yet hit the tips of the Amargosas. He stood on my front step, his work clothes coated with silt. A bruise colored his chin and cheek, and he held a red bandanna to his face. When he lifted the cloth, I saw one of his eyes was swollen shut.

"God, B! What happened?"

He waved me off. "We've got to get going."

"Where?"

"We can talk on the way."

First I packed ice from my freezer into a plastic bag. "Not without this."

We started off in the pre-dawn air, with his jeep's soft top rolled up and me at the wheel. B iced his face as I drove and snuck looks at him. "Did Barry and Jerry work you over?"

He groaned in pain. "I stepped on the rake I use to clean out my pool. The wooden handle flew up and hit me in the face. Hard."

"Oh, good one. 'Man Attacked by Garden Tool.'"

He grinned, then winced. "Ow. Don't make me laugh."

We rolled up to the one stop sign in town on Highway 127. Turning left would lead us to B's spring. Turning right would take us to Badwater, out in Death Valley.

"Go right," he said.

I cranked the wheel. The road to Badwater stretched out before us. The rearview mirror filled with the first rays of sunlight that would soon burst over the Kingstons.

After a few miles, B said, "I'm such an idiot."

"How so?"

"Barry and Jerry did come looking for me." He moved the ice pack. "And that thing they were building? A tub for water. A beautiful object. They'd meant to make it for Rebecca years ago. It's even engraved."

"Engraved?"

"Yeah. With two words."

"Let me guess. It says, 'Golden Rule.'"

"No," he said. "No. 'The Wish.'"

Tears wet my cheeks. B didn't notice, I don't think, with that icepack still on his face. We kept on, arriving at the salt flats near Badwater just as the sun broke above the horizon. Light hit the tops of the Panamint Mountains to the west. Their peaks blushed pink. More light flowed into the valley, the warmth of the sun taking the edge off the night's chill. On the flats a web of mudcracks reached out from the edge of the parking lot where we stood.

B's swelling had gone down a little. He shaded his eyes as the mud came into the sun. Then we heard it: a single, small pop. Silence followed, then a snap, sudden as a snare rim shot, random as popping corn.

I turned to B, my eyes wide.

He looked happy. He put his arms around me and stood close. His heart beat against my ribs. "It's the salt crystals. They break as the mud warms and expands. It means there's water in the layers. Talking to us."

"Singing to us."

When the sun came full on the flats, the mudcrack choir went wild. It didn't last long, slowing to one pop every ten seconds, then one every half minute, then less. When it stopped altogether, I faced B for a long embrace. Taking our time we eventually moved apart, then made our way back to the jeep, where we rolled down the top. With me driving again, B spilled actual tears.

"Okay," was all he said.

He kept weeping, and I just let him, figuring he'd have to let it out. He'd have to let it flow. There was nothing to do but hold the wheel and think of the music as we followed the highway back to where we started and at the same time farther along.

An Exposition of the Development of the Earth

.   .   .

Near the end of his life, my maternal grandfather pulled me into the middle of his story. "Thank you for beginning your new book *in media res*, Mare," he wrote. As always, his penciled cursive slanted to the right; it almost floated off the page, so light was his hand. "In *Dryland* (superb title), I'm hooked from the first scene. *Brava!*" Using perfect grammar and complete sentences, he detailed his admiration for my second environmental crime novel ("outdoor murder mystery," he called it, "starring your alter ego 'Reb'"). His letter outlined evidence of his close reading. Then, after three chatty pages, he asked, "something near to my heart. I'm finishing a scientific treatise on the formation of the Earth. Can you help me complete it?"

I telephoned my mother Joan, B.S. Stanford, M.S. Princeton, Ph.D. Berkeley, professor of Earth Sciences at UCLA, and my grandfather's only child. She had just a minute to talk. She sighed, an exhalation no doubt forcing out the ubiquitous cloud from a cigarette. "You'd smoke, too, if you lived in L.A.," she once told me. "It's recreational, Mare. Like your river trips."

I brought up Grandpa's request. "Have you read his work?"

"Glanced at it. He theorizes an accelerating Earth. Quite unique."

"He says he needs help."

"Well, at age eighty-five . . . "

Perhaps she was looking out her window then, thinking of her father's growing frailty. Time had whittled him down so his shirts appeared bigger every year. "Wish I could lend a hand, but my course load already keeps me in irons. Besides." She laughed. "You know how wary he is of institutions. To him, I'm one of the 'educated idiots.' You, on the other hand, being both a boater and published author, are held in high esteem. Oh God! Look at the time. Mare, hon, I've got to go teach."

Saying good-bye to the already silent line, I hung up and dialed Grandpa's number. If I called through the time zones any later, he and Grandma would be watching M.A.S.H. reruns, which they'd never abandon for a ringing phone.

Grandma picked up, her voice quavering as it had for years. "Al's in the barn loft. Hang on, I'll get him." She set down the handset with a light tap. I envisioned her bowed walk to the back door to find her husband of five decades, her customary cardigan thrown over bony shoulders. I checked my watch once, then again. I was due to pick up my son Sammy at school.

"Hi, girl." Grandpa answered minutes later, his breath labored. "Sorry to keep you waiting. There's no fast way down those steps."

He queued up his question with care, as if building a long-needed bridge. In his opinion, scientists hadn't "adequately described the mechanism" to explain the presence of similar fossils on separate continents. "And my work does. I just need help completing it—and publishing it. That's where you come in, Mare. We'd be co-authors."

"Grandpa, I'm no scientist. I write novels—I spin them out of thin air."

"Exactly!" His slight lisp grew stronger. "You have a keen sense of story. That's critical to good science writing. You must have drawn on technical sources for *Extinction*. Very convincing."

My cheeks filled with blood. My grandfather didn't know how much I'd pulled my first novel from imagination.

"Besides," he said, "you have another equally important qualification."

"Which is?"

"You're published. You know what it takes to get into print."

"Do you have a journal in mind?"

"*S_____ Magazine,* of course. Top of the line for work like this. And Mare, in case you need incentive, your mother said you'd like to have my guideboat. Help me with this, and it's yours."

"Blackmail! Grandpa, I hate to rush, but I have to get Sammy at school. Send me your paper, okay? I'll take a look."

"Thanks, girl." His voice sounded both fierce and fragile. "You're a good one."

Replacing the receiver, I stared at it a moment before running out the door, car keys in hand.

• • •

My grandfather's guideboat was the only thing of his I coveted. I'd admired it since my teens, when I'd learned to pull a pair of oars: it was as narrow as a canoe, braced inside with curved ribs, and fitted with brass oarlocks like a dory. Guideboats had been the craft of choice in upstate New York in the first half of the twentieth century, after which the boats had dwindled in number. They were rare anywhere, but especially out West—all the more reason I wanted to drive one home to Utah someday.

This particular guideboat was a bit of an anomaly. Built by Fred Rice, it was found wrecked and abandoned on a lake in the Adirondacks where my grandfather worked as a summer guide. "Rice was the best craftsman," said Grandpa. "Everyone wanted his boats." Being a skilled woodworker himself, and a man who'd fished from everything that floats, Grandpa rebuilt the guideboat using home-milled wood and fiberglass. The synthetic material might have raised eyebrows in the purists' circle, but I didn't question it. If he believed a hull needed resin and glass, it did. Through the years he used the boat most weekends, exploring little strings of lakes and escaping to the quiet world of fishing.

He'd never before raised the subject of who should inherit the guideboat when the time came. Joan and I had described it to the Adirondack Museum during a visit, thinking a Rice boat belonged there, but the specialists doubted the historical value of a boat patched with fiberglass. Until the phone call about his manuscript, I had never considered that I might bring Grandpa's legacy West.

Since his eyes had clouded at age seventy, he had relied on others to row him, resigning himself to passenger status. I'd been the latest guest at his oars, having flown to Rochester alone while my husband Jack stayed home with Sammy. Driving south to Geneseo through a golden autumn, I followed the hushed river. As always I calmed with every mile of distance from the airport. Pulling into my grandparents' neighborhood, I took solace in the piles of yellow and orange leaves on the lawns and the unfenced backyards with gardens bearing the season's last vegetables. Inside my grandparents' two-story former farmhouse, smoke lingered from their decades-old cigarette habits. I carried my things to the upstairs bedroom that had been theirs in earlier years, opening a window to let in fresh air.

Next morning Grandpa and I launched the guideboat on a farm reservoir outside town. He sat on the bow seat, facing me with outstretched legs. The double-ended hull glided through the water as if new. Grandpa searched shore, his eyes perhaps taking in the colors of the changing woods but not distinguishing species of tree as they once had.

"My eyesight's really shot," he said. "I wonder what ability I'll lose next."

Sunlight filtered through a fall haze. I rowed the lake's perimeter, smelling the sweetness of decaying leaves. A loon called across the water.

"Hear that?" Grandpa put a hand behind one of his enormous ears. "Migrant. Passes through every year. Used to be little flocks of them, but now we just get one or two." We listened for more. Silence.

After a minute, he said, "Tell me how you learned about species loss."

I shook my head. "I know hardly anything."

"But in *Extinction,* your protagonist Reb weighs the importance of her own life against that of the Ivory-Billed Woodpecker. What inspired her thinking?" He scanned the shoreline, as if he could make out detail.

"Just a hunch. I get the urge to give up on living when a species winks out."

He swung his gaze toward me, his foggy eyes wide.

"Don't worry." I forced a grin. "I won't act on it."

He didn't smile. "We have to persevere constantly, Mare. We have to—" The loon called again. "There! Like the loon. We have to stick with it year after year."

My head throbbed, growing achy. I closed my eyes, still rowing, until Grandpa warned me I was off course. Readjusting for another time around the small lake, I felt my face flush. It would be bad form, indeed, to run ashore.

Back near my grandfather's Chevy Impala, we disembarked, gripped the gunnels of the boat, and swung it to the roof racks. My head pounded as I bore most of the weight of the lifting. Still, it was Grandpa who groaned and bent forward in pain. He couldn't hide his pale face and set lips as he waved off my concern.

He said, "It comes and goes."

We drove back to town through rolling drumlin valleys dotted with old farms and scattered new homes. Grandpa's presence beside me felt transient in a way it never had all the summers I'd spent with him and Grandma—he was thinner, ghost like.

In a slight voice, he said, "You're a good driver, Mare. An accomplished oarswoman, too. I think you're ready for that boat."

I didn't respond. If I spoke, I'd want to tell him something he might find sentimental: that I craved the boat now because it carried the light of a fall day and the memory of him riding in the bow.

◆ ◆ ◆

Grandpa's manuscript arrived on a Friday afternoon in November. My family and I were preparing for a weekend away—Sammy and Jack had been packing a bag of plastic trucks while I cleared the clutter of a week's work from my desk. We didn't see that the mailman had come and gone from our porch until Jack spotted a package through the glass-paned front door.

He brought me a box addressed in pencil, cursive letters slanting right. Lifting tape, I stripped away brown-paper wrapping from an ancient, black binder. Its pressed-cardboard cover bore my grandfather's full name in stamped gold. I ran my fingers over each letter before flipping the cover open to a manuscript of onionskin pages. Crisp and professional looking, they must have been prepared by Grandma, who'd worked as a typist for thirty years—errors, if there were any, would have been lifted by the erasure tape in her trusted Selectric. She no longer used the manual 1942 Royal she still owned and that I'd tapped on as a kid, one clacking keystroke after another.

The first page, and the title, lay before me: "Accelerating Rotation Theory: An Exposition of the Development of the Earth."

Jack stuck his head into my office. His hair stood up in bunches, as it did when he'd been playing with Sammy.

"How's Al's paper look?"

"Impressive."

"Why not bring it this weekend? Read it in the cabin."

"I don't dare take this anywhere. Jack, listen to this."

Night and day are generally thought of as passing around the Earth once during each period of rotation, which of course they do. Day remains always on the Earth's sunward side and night on its opposite dark hemisphere, which in fact they do. With this in mind, it is readily understood that the evolution of life, inseparable from the processes of erosion and sedimentation, occurred only on the Earth's sunlit hemisphere until shortening of the day-night cycle established climatic conditions about as they are today.

"Huh," said Jack. "Make a copy. Got to run, we're trying to decide whether to pack Teddy or Piggy . . . "

I slipped the manuscript from the binder. Stacking it for my fax/copier, I didn't take my eyes off the machine as it worked. The copies came out dark but legible, its black letters standing out against each page like lifebuoys against fog. I clicked the originals back into the binder and carried it with care to our fire safe. Our house deed, our family trusts, and my original book manuscripts were now joined by a discourse on a planet that Grandpa theorized became itself through swifter and swifter rotation.

.   .   .

Over the weekend I felt drawn to those photocopies like a needle pulled north. The manuscript had the quality of creation myth, with careful words in an unfamiliar language. My grandfather's story drew me—it didn't matter that I might not grasp its meaning—but I let it alone while I immersed in life with Jack and Sammy.

What good fortune that I had a loving family and minimal drama, unlike Reb in my novels. Brilliant about her work in forensics, biology, and anthropology, she would have no problem dissecting the meaning of Grandpa's treatise with the sharpness of a Samurai sword. Her good thinking, however, wouldn't include keeping her personal life on track. Reb conducted a series of bad romances, was estranged from her parents, had a wayward daughter, and made no time for friends—in short, she lived a train-wreck of a life. It was more like the regular trauma I had lived with in my river-guide years, before my friendship with Jack had matured into love.

After putting Sammy to bed, while an early snow brushed the windows of the cabin, I read passages to Jack.

> In late pre-Cambrian time, through a process as yet unknown, forms of life materialized among the sediments on the floor of the pri-mordial sea. Their fossilized remains are found in several unconformably deposited rock strata common to all of the continents. From this evi-dence, it is deduced that the Earth made several rotations during which time the primordial sea remained on its sunward side before the ocean basins were formed and into which the ancient sea gravitated.

He thought a minute. "Does it make sense to you?"

"It has such . . . authority. You want to believe him. But it sounds so unlikely."

"As in imaginary?" Jack reached up to draw a curtain over the whitening window.

"Like my fiction."

"Maybe he needs technical help." He put his arms around me. "And his time's growing short. Can you call Joan next week?"

I sighed as we curled together in bed, Jack's heartbeat steady against my back.

• • •

Monday descended, then evaporated in a slew of editorial calls. Evening had settled before I could try Joan. When I did telephone her, she answered and agreed to review Grandpa's material with me. I read aloud:

> Referring now specifically to animal life, certain invertebrates attained mobility and "marked time" among the sediments on the floor of that ancient sunward sea. The calcareous remains of their dead ancestors were carried, as on an endless belt, through the night environment of the Earth's opposite side. When that floor (the surface of any given continent) returned each time into the day environment, the nucleus of life which was marking time there had evolved and in some instances entirely new forms had appeared.

Joan coughed. "In a way, it's brilliant. He describes conveyer-belt transport as part of evolutionary design. But he doesn't integrate the sea-floor spreading that's been well documented since the 1970s. There's no mention of plate tectonics."

"Does Grandpa even believe in plate tectonics?"

She hemmed. "He wouldn't be alone if he didn't. A few very accomplished researchers refute it. But I'm afraid he's barking up trees cut down a long time ago."

My heart took a dive. A moment passed.

Joan asked, "Are you there?"

"Yeah." My voice came out small, an echo from the summers of my youth. Over all a quiet but vital grandfather had presided in sun hat, fishing vest, and rubber boots.

My mother and I spoke a bit more before saying goodbye. I carried Grandpa's treatise to the living room, where Jack and Sammy were finishing a game of Rummy. Sammy applauded when he saw the binder.

"Great-Grandpa's story! Can we read it for bedtime?"

I shook my head. "It's still being worked on."

"Please!" Sammy jumped up.

"It's not a good kid's book."

"I'm not a kid!" All four feet of my son bounced on our couch.

"Sammy, what did we say about furniture?" Jack asked.

"Please." Sammy jumped to the floor, his eyes on me.

Jack held his cards near his chin, waiting.

"Well. Only if you're in bed in a flash, Sammy-O." I fanned my fingers in our signal meaning *five minutes.* He ran to brush his teeth.

Jack set down his Rummy hand. "What'd Joan say?"

"That Al has missed the boat. No pun intended."

"It's not good science?"

"I imagine it's the absolute best a woodworker-slash-fisherman living in a town of one thousand can do with references from the public library."

He frowned. "What's next?"

"I have to tell Al something. I'm not sure what." I kissed Jack's standing-up hair and took the binder into Sammy's room. Settling on his bed, I reclined with my son on a throne of pillows. He clutched his stuffed pig, his little chest rising and falling from his rushed nighttime routine.

I opened Grandpa's binder to the introduction. "You ready?"

"Of course!"

"Here's something from near the beginning. 'There came a time when some amphibians'—that means frogs and newts—"

"Duh."

"'... evolved to an existence entirely terrestrial.' That means they moved from living in the ocean to being on land."

"Wow!"

"'Some of the reptiles—you know, snakes and lizards—"

"Double duh."

"Sorry. '... attained improved means and methods of mobilization.' He's saying they could walk around pretty well once they became land creatures."

Sammy raised one hand in the air.

"Yes, Sammy?"

"Great-Grandpa Al is smart, isn't he, Mom?"

"Very."

My all-knowing son sat up, nowhere near sleepy.

"Mom, what's 'evolved'?"

◆　◆　◆

Two days later I arrived home from grocery shopping to a ringing phone. I hurried to my office in time to hear the message machine recording, "... his number at the hospital is ... "

I picked up. "Grandma?"

"There you are, Mare. It's that pain again. He was out with Chuck gathering hickory nuts until his chest hurt. Got 'tighter than a table vise,' he said. He came home wheezing like our fireplace bellows. *Eeh-haw. Eeh-haw.* I took him to Dansville. Your mother knows."

I had visited the massive brick Noyes Hospital in Dansville only once, when I was twelve or so. Joan and I'd gone to see ninety-eight-year-old Auntie Gev, who'd lost the desire to eat or drink. Her chin-length hair was paper white, and her clear, blue gaze reminded me of creek water. The biggest clue that she was failing was her voice, which possessed far more air than sound. My mother had to lean in to hear as I watched the green of trees outside the window and wondered how soon we could leave.

Now, when I telephoned Grandpa's room, he spoke with that same hush Gev had all those years ago. "They're running a few more tests on me. Then I'm going home."

"You take it easy. Don't do the Grandpa thing and act all stubborn."

He chuckled, then gasped as if struck. I waited as he labored to breathe.

When his discomfort passed, I said, "Grandpa, I read your treatise. It's very well written. Jack and Sammy like it, too."

"Can you . . . do anything with it?" His breath ebbed and flowed.

"Well, it's so good, but so technical."

"Right, girl. That's where you come in."

"You mean interpret it?" I sighed. "I doubt I can. It's beyond my abilities."

Silence. Then, "Well, you can have the boat anyway. I won't be using it."

"Grandpa, I—"

I stopped to listen as his handset rocked and scrabbled on the cradle before settling in.

A recording came on, telling me to hang up if I'd like to make a call. My thoughts first ran cool with indignation then warm with a desire to somehow rescue him in some brilliant way. I dialed my grandmother. She listened to

my bruised account of Grandpa's dismissal, then asked,
"Is it publishable, Mare?"

"Well . . . "

"Ah," she said. "You know, he sent it to *S_____ Magazine* a few years ago. It took them months to respond."

"And?"

"They sent a letter back saying his idea had no merit
whatsoever." Her thin voice shook. "They didn't have to
say that. It was just—mean. He was so mad he didn't speak
for days. Oh, he'd shut me out before, but not for years."

"Now I'm in for the silent treatment."

"Yes." She paused. "Mare, I wish people knew how hard
he's worked. Twenty years, off and on. Reading late at
night, spending weekends at the library . . . he's been at it
far longer than the average person spends in college."

"Or even getting a doctorate."

"Oh?" She chuckled as she did when she hadn't quite
heard. "You know, he's very intelligent. He would've
been an important man out West if he hadn't been called
home."

"Out West? When?"

"During the Depression. You didn't know?" Her words
came bit by bit, pulled out of deep memory. My grandfather had helped survey the last unmapped sections of the
Grand Canyon, Arizona, and Mount Lassen, California.
He had a letter of commendation from the U.S. Geological Survey.

Grandma said, "Major Dutton signed it himself. We still
have the letter upstairs. I wish *S_____ Magazine* knew
that."

"Who called him home?"

My great-grandfather—to me just a face in a sepia-
toned photograph—was about to lose the family farm.

He demanded his third son come home. All hands were needed, or they'd lose the land.

"His grandfather claimed the loss it would be on Al's head," Grandma said. "It wasn't fair, and it hit him hard. We should never ask such things of our children."

. . .

The next day I spoke with my agent. "Victoria, who do we know at *S_____ Magazine?*"

"Nobody, but I can find someone who does. What's up?"

"I want to get a story on their back page."

"Mare, the back page? I'm pretty sure they don't do fiction."

"This is different. I have a . . . piece about loyalty and family history. Can you call me if it's a go?"

"Absolutely."

Next I dialed the hospital. When I reached Grandpa's room, Joan answered. She'd flown to Rochester, driven to Dansville, and was at his bedside.

"He's sleeping now," she whispered.

"I have to talk to him. It's his exposition. I have an idea for it—to get it in print. But it would be different, a little. What I need to know is, would it be okay to give it a new twist?"

"Yes. Yes, I'm sure it would. But Mare, he's very sick."

"How sick?"

"He's got cancer—lung cancer. And he's refusing treatment."

The words fell hard, a tower toppling.

Joan continued, "He's probably not going home."

My mind went to memories of muggy summer days, with barbecues near warm ponds. My cousins and I swam with our feet held high to avoid the muddy bottom and the leeches we were certain were there. We played dress-up with Grandma's steamer trunks of dress-up clothes, racked up countless games of dominoes, and rushed around the lawns that surrounded my grandparents' big, wood-frame house until fireflies traced ephemeral loops in the dark.

"Mare? He says you're to receive his guideboat. 'No arguments,' he told me."

"But—"

"The doctor just arrived. Sorry, hon, got to run. Talk later?"

Leaving my office, I crossed through the house to our bedroom, fell on the bed, and wept into an afghan my Grandma had crocheted for a wedding present. By the time Jack brought Sammy home, I hadn't moved. My husband and son stood in the doorway, puzzled looks on their faces. Then Sammy ran to watch a cartoon while Jack started a pizza baking.

Jack returned to sit with me, his hazel eyes as dark as they get. With his mouth set in a line, he listened to my news. He asked, "Can you fly there this week?"

"Yeah. I'll check for tickets first thing tomorrow."

He rubbed my back. "What's happening with *S_____ Magazine?*"

"Victoria thinks she can get me in. I want to adapt a piece from his . . . " I resumed weeping.

Jack reached an arm around me. "Mare, babe, you need dinner. Come on. Pizza's ready."

After picking at my meal, I roamed the house, looking out windows into our circle of woods. It had been a dry winter. Our garden lay bare and hummocky from light snows that had melted without sticking. I closed my eyes. When I reopened them, I considered the indoor furniture: a drop-leaf table and chairs made by Grandpa; a recipe box built of his signature cherry wood; a walking cane carved from a pine branch he'd collected in the forests outside his hometown. In my office, two pictures of him stood on my bookshelf. One showed him linking arms with Grandma on their fiftieth wedding anniversary, she tiny and wearing a sky-blue cardigan over her shoulders, he heads higher in a short-sleeved cotton shirt. In the second photo, Grandpa strolled through red-and-yellow woods by the Genesee River. He wore his fall coat and flannel-lined khaki pants. Anyone who didn't know better would think he was just a random old man closing the distance.

Letting my hand roam the spines of books, I pulled out my novel *Extinction*. I opened it, by chance coming to this passage near the middle:

> It wasn't that the birds were gone that turned
> her off to the human race; it was that we had
> killed them. Ivory-Billed Woodpeckers had only
> wanted a chance to further their DNA and raise
> their young in a couple of swamps in Louisiana.
> In the game of survival of the fittest, they held
> a losing hand. Now some murderer was out
> there, targeting ornithologists who protected
> the Ivory Bill legacy, and Reb intended to find
> him or die trying.

I slapped the book shut.

Sitting at my desk, I took up my notebook and favorite roller-ball pen. I flipped through Grandpa's binder, searching for key words: *changes, processes, transformation. Exposition.* Sketching circles and curves in my notebook, I let my scribbling develop into phrases, then sentences.

On the page in front of me, a story was taking shape.

. . .

In the morning, Grandpa's voice on the phone came from
a faraway place. Even as he murmured, I heard stubborn-
ness in the rising inflection of his sentences.

"No chemo for me," he said.

My blood raced. "But . . . you said we have to stick with
it. Year after year."

He let out the world's weariest sigh.

"Remember that loon?" I asked. "What happened to 'we
have to persevere constantly'?"

"I have been." His voice was as faint as a light breeze.
"Over eighty years of it."

"Grandpa. My agent is getting your—our work—into
S_____ Magazine." I wanted to add, "those bastards," but
did not.

"Good girl."

"I'm flying out to see you tomorrow."

"Do," he said. "Bring your family, Mare. You can take
them out in the boat."

We finished our call, and I stared out the window at
the blue Utah sky. A wisp of cloud gathered over mountains to the east. After several minutes, I wiped my
damp eyes with both shirtsleeves before turning on my
computer. Calling up a new document, I drummed my
fingers on the edge of the keyboard, thinking. With time,
a technical paper might evolve from my grandfather's
manuscript. Meanwhile I would write the kind of prose I
knew best.

Sammy wandered in, wearing Grandma's crocheted
afghan as a cape.

"Mom, can I—what are you doing?

"Typing a story. Great-Grandpa Al's story."

"From his book? That beginning part?"

"Not really. This starts more in the middle. It takes place in the wild West when there were no maps yet, just giant birds and bears and big villages of really wise native people."

"Is Great-Grandpa in it?"

I nodded. "He climbed tall mountains and crossed untamed rivers with other daring explorers."

"Cool!"

Sammy ran off, satisfied with my answer and forgetting whatever he'd come in to ask. I typed through the day, taking no breaks except for dinner, returning to my desk after dark. While I drafted sentences and shaped paragraphs, I heard Jack's voice carrying through the house—no doubt spinning bedtime tales for Sammy about our son's new favorite subject, Great-Grandpa the hero. Even after the murmur of storytelling had ended and Jack had gone to bed himself, the words poured out of me onto the page. As I wrote late, my lamp no doubt illuminated the only work-in-progress in Utah that included a guideboat, an important man from Geneseo, and an exposition of the development of the Earth.

Endangered Species

. . .

If I were to make a study of the tracks
of animals and represent them by plates,
I should conclude with the tracks of man.
—Henry David Thoreau

The Pomeranian next door must have turned prey in an instant. One minute his yapping hovered near Tom's consciousness, the next the dog squealed as if skewered. Terror filled the momentary high-pitched scream, cut off mid breath, followed by silence. Anybody out doing yard work, as Tom was, would've heard it. Certainly the birds did—a murder of crows cawed up from the big Doug-fir. They flushed and settled again, and the sunset-pink air grew quiet. Tom froze in place, a wave of brown hair in his eyes. When he heard nothing more, he checked over the fence but saw only his neighbor Martin's perfect green lawn, potted pink geraniums, and hot tub protected with padded red top.

About an hour after the dog's disappearance, with Tom still working as dusk settled, he heard Martin calling for his pet from the back steps. There was no answer, least of all the pig-like snuffles the dog made when excited. The Pomeranian had been in the habit of wandering to the creek, and Martin called again near its banks. Still no reply.

"Tom, my man." Martin peered at him through the small gap between their fences. "Is Pommie with you by any chance?"

"Haven't seen him."

From a distance and in dim light, Martin looked younger than his sixty-two years, but up close, his true age became obvious. The sharp boundary stood out between his auburn hair dye and white sideburns. His facial skin looked somehow stretched beyond its normal elasticity. When they'd met, Martin had confided to Tom that he'd just had his "eyes done" and that his interest in playing golf was only to stay fit enough to date women thirty years his junior.

"In other words, women around your age, my man. Although I'm no longer as handsome as you."

Martin retreated inside, and Tom resumed hacking a stand of bay laurel grown out of control. He was getting his parents' northern California home ready to sell. When his mother had fallen ill, he'd driven up from Vegas for what he thought would be a long visit. Instead she passed on within days, followed a month later by his father who hadn't been healthy for years. Tom proceeded to take care of details, all the while missing his folks as well as his wife, Sue, who'd just filed for divorce after a long separation.

In the morning Martin reported his dog's disappearance to sheriff's office and the Pets Ahoy Animal Shelter. Both warned that there'd been recent mountain lion sightings and he should call Fish and Game about the incident. Martin did, then let Tom know that a warden would come out in the afternoon. Tom didn't hesitate. He took his little digital point-and-shoot to the creek to look for tracks. He had hunted when he was younger but lately had made the move from Remington to Canon. Although he'd lost the urge to kill, he still liked the stealth needed to close in on wildlife and capture their beauty.

Tom skirted the fence line to the channel. The ground felt dry and firm until he reached the water. There the bed gave way underfoot, muddy and soft, and the air smelled of wet earth. The creek trickled at its October low—not much flow before the rains started for the season.

Years earlier, he had loved walking the creek up into the hills. Less than a mile from his parents' back gate, he found dark redwood groves and deep stands of oak draped with lichen. The woods were untamed, unplanned—perfect to Tom's eyes. The creek tumbled over falls and ledges of black rock. Up there he found sharp-edged deer prints, heron tracks scrabbled in the mud, and raccoon scat full of crawdad shells. Along the creek he felt a rare peace. It reminded him of the hushed sanctuary of the church he and Sue had attended on the north coast.

Behind Martin's house, a walkthrough steel culvert underlay a bridge crossing for his long, paved driveway, which continued beside a row of Italian cypress. The stream ran between concrete embankments, where a pipe poured spring water out among fern and monkey flower. Martin had built a holding pool, square and stylish. No doubt it attracted wildlife despite its intended purpose, which was, Martin said, "to astonish his out-of-town guests with its upscale design."

Now, carrying his camera, Tom spotted what he was looking for among the patches of stream gravel: a single animal print, no less than six inches across, four splayed toe pads in an impression as detailed as a plaster cast. The fifth and central pad resembled a flattened human nose—rounded with two wings flaring like nostrils. The whole thing was deep, pressed into the mud with authority. There were no claw marks showing.

Lion print. Still filling with water. If it was the predator who'd attacked Pommie the Pomeranian, it had come back.

Tom acted fast, snapping photos, making sure to capture the print near his own foot for scale. When he'd documented it to his satisfaction, he looked for others. Nothing. It appeared the animal had moved on hard bedrock when it could. Tom used his toe to scrape some pebbles over the single track as well as his own footprints—with care, to leave no trace.

As he made his way back toward home, a breeze brought the pungent smell of soaked fur. More scent came, strong and rank: big cat odor? Tom's heart pumped with excitement, but he also felt the fear of being prey. He made himself as big as possible by raising his jacket above his head and singing Green Day songs so loud his chest rattled. It took him only a minute or so to back downstream and scramble up the bank to his garden.

• • •

Later that day, the Fish and Game warden arrived and stood with Tom and Martin overlooking the creek. A tall man with a tan uniform, orange safety vest, and shaved head, he hunkered near an Italian cypress and advised. "Don't go down there alone. And never at dawn or dusk, when predators hunt. You don't want to run into one—no way, no how."

Martin asked, "What about my Pommie?"

The warden shook his head. "Sorry, sir. If it was a lion, it's protected—an endangered species." He handed Martin a brochure entitled *Living in Cougar Country*.

Martin snorted.

The warden eyed him. "I'll check back in a week or so. Or you can call me anytime. Name's Brad."

Brad handed them each his business card. "And don't worry. More people are hit by lightning than killed by lions. You follow the advice in that pamphlet, you'll be fine."

Tom returned to the kitchen at his folks' place, where he'd set up his laptop. For a minute he thought about not printing the photos he'd taken of the animal track. As he deliberated, the phone rang, and it was Martin. He'd just invited his "woman friend" to visit from Los Angeles. He couldn't stand to be alone, "especially with Pommie gone. It's been terrible, just terrible."

The friend, a freelance portrait photographer, would arrive in a few days. "You and Trudy will have a lot to talk about, both being artists of the lens."

"But I'm just an amateur."

"Oh but you're good at everything—your dear old folks, rest their souls, told me so." Martin lowered his voice, as if anyone would be listening. "Confidentially, Tom, I hope to marry Trudy, though she's younger and still busy with her career."

"You haven't asked her?"

"Soon," Martin said. "The time has to be right."

Tom signed off and sat back down to print out just one photo of the animal track. Then he spent the afternoon clearing more of the unpruned growth out back of the house.

◆ ◆ ◆

Over the next two days, Tom observed Martin sparing no effort tidying up his yard for Trudy's arrival. His mow-and-blow guy came to do the lawn, but instead of ignoring the man as he usually did, Martin directed him to rewrap his Italian cypress in mist nets from the lowest branches to the conical tops. When finished, the trees in silhouette looked like dark-green, narrow-headed people.

In the evenings Tom read news websites online. The town's *Journal-Tribune* had run a series on local wildlife, and readers had posted more than thirty comments. Landowners on several hillside properties had seen "a large creature, moving fast" and a "tawny animal that jumped the fence." The comments culminated at the bottom of the webpage with this one:

Dear Editor,

We live on the creek and personally observe wild animals from the surrounding hills using the waterway as a sort of "sidewalk" into town. This would be fine except some are fierce predators that will stop at nothing to get their needs met. I've already lost my beloved pet to some stalking beast. It could just as well have been a small child carried off! Then wouldn't the community be in an uproar! Now there are reports of mountain lions roaming the hills. A

coincidence? I think not. My question to city
officials is, how far will you let this situation go
on before you act?

Sincerely, Martin Banks

Tom's heart beat hard as he considered responding
with what he knew.

Later that day Martin brought Trudy over with her
camera. Her blonde hair shone in the sunshine, and her
light brown eyes showed mixed excitement and caution.
The color in her cheeks deepened as Martin made intro-
ductions. A moment later he excused himself to return a
phone call to an "Indiana Jones type" who was going to
help him with something.

"Your yard is lovely." Trudy hoisted her camera. "Mind
if I . . . ?"

Tom shrugged.

She snapped pictures of the ash grove, of the maple
losing its leaves, and of Tom ripping English ivy off an oak
tree, where the vine had taken hold.

She said, "This place feels so natural."

Tom nodded. "My parents put in only native plants.
And they never used any chemicals. They were . . . " His
voice caught. " . . . ahead of their time."

She gave him a sympathetic look, then checked her
camera. "Here," she said, showing him the digital viewer.

He looked first to be polite and then from real interest.
Each of her shots was insightful. There were close-ups
of leaf patterns, wide-angle views of plant assemblages
with the artistry of mosaics, and details of Doug-fir cones
scattered like runes on homebuilt rock walls.

"You've got a good eye," he said, as Martin returned.

Martin beamed and tapped his forehead. "Vision. It's what Trudy brings to the *table*."

"Oh, Martin." Trudy sighed.

"I'm serious," he said. "Only you could find beauty in this overgrown jungle."

She blushed again. "It *is* beautiful. And it's *not* a jungle."

Martin put an arm around her shoulders and said goodbye, then walked her toward his yard. Tom didn't look up from his ivy pulling until they'd neared the house, where Martin let Trudy go as she turned to snap his containers of French lavender and Russian sage. Tom thought she might glance his way before going inside, but it was Martin who darted a look back at him.

• • •

Trudy returned alone the next afternoon, slipping unannounced through the gap between the fences.

"Martin was called away on last-minute business," she said, moving her camera aside as she helped pull weeds. "The money was too good to pass up."

When she continued working without gloves, Tom offered his. She took them and peered at him. "Martin doesn't garden. He hires somebody to help. But you probably knew that."

They worked side by side, Tom silent, Trudy humming. He felt light headed, having her so close by. He counted the months since Sue had left him over that mess with the stripper from the Sapphire in Vegas. Eleven months— almost a year. Christ.

When the sun dropped near the hills, Trudy straightened up and removed the gloves. "Have you seen the creature Martin thinks got Pommie?"

"No." Tom didn't look up from his work.

"Was it a mountain lion, do you think?"

He shrugged.

She persisted. "I'd like to see it."

He stopped weeding to look at her. "Why?"

Her shining eyes excited him, but he tried not to let it show. No way he would reveal much to any woman again, not since he'd begged Sue to come back with no success. He'd driven to that desert town where she worked and said he'd take all the blame. How could he have known that he'd leave their home on the coast, hit the blue skies of Nevada, and lose all sense? But Sue had said he'd made his bed and could damn well lie in it.

Tom eyed Trudy. "Because you wouldn't want to be closer to any predator than . . . well, no closer than looking down from your rooftop."

"Great idea! Let's get the ladder. Maybe we'll see something."

He excused himself to grab his camera, then met her at Martin's double-car garage, where her Volkswagen beetle was parked by itself. He set up the extension ladder as she directed against the back gutter of Martin's house.

"Martin wouldn't do this." She giggled.

She preceded Tom up the ladder and over the gutter. He held the rungs, watching her camera swing above her jeans as she climbed. Once she reached the roof, she held the top of the ladder for him. Her grip was firm, solid.

From the sloping asphalt shingles, they had a clear view of an unclouded western horizon. A strip of gold lingered over the hills. Upstream of Martin's cypress and spring, the creek wound out of sight. Trudy snapped photo after photo; Tom took a few shots, too, mostly of her bright-toothed, almost maniacal joy. Dark settled. Stars followed in a moonless sky.

"I'm not afraid of the predator," Trudy said. "Whatever it is. But Martin really fears it."

"He should."

She laughed. "Serious?"

Tom shrugged.

"You're so funny," she said. "Not like anyone else I know."

The air grew colder, with a hint of marine layer drifting in from the coast. Tom and Trudy sat close but not touching until they agreed it was time to go back down. She retreated to Martin's big house on a path well illuminated with sensor lights. Tom strode with purposeful steps toward his parents' narrow walkway through the unlit native garden and inside to the old hide-a-bed.

Over the next two evenings, with Martin detained by business, Tom and Trudy climbed to the roof again. The second night resembled the first, clear and mild followed by a slow chill. Trudy brought a fleece throw and Tom was glad she did, because the damp, cool air got to his bones, as it had when he and Sue had lived on the coast. White tufts of fog hung on the western hills, sunlight cutting the mist tops as if slicing smoke. Oaks rattled in the wind down by the creek and, as darkness came on, black tree limbs framed by gray evening faded into night.

"It's beautiful," she said. "Those sun rays looked like heaven."

"Uh-huh. Bet you and your camera captured it."

She leaned close. "What I want to capture is the predator."

He turned. They lay back in each other's arms.

"We should go in," she said. "Together."

"Your fiancé wouldn't like that."

"Fiancé?" She giggled. "More like sugar daddy."

"He doesn't see it that way, I'll bet. No, I'd best head home."

He didn't see her all the next day until they rendez-voused in the evening. This time they spent sunset on the roof wrapped in Tom's Hudson Bay blanket. They traded just a few more words about Martin.

"He hates the predator," she said, hand on Tom's belly.

"Why? She—or he—is just a lone animal coming to the spring."

She stiffened. "Martin's spring?"

Tom pulled away. "I'm only guessing."

"You've seen something."

"I didn't say that. Look, we'd better call it a night. You're cold."

"Yes. All of a sudden."

The next morning, she joined him in the back garden, where he was picking native blackberries. She looked exhausted, her eyes shadowed with dark gray rings.

"Tom, you're killing me."

He stopped his work. "How?"

"Why won't you come inside?"

"I'm still married. And you almost are."

She studied a berry as if it held an answer. "They're so filled with dark juice." She looked up and ran her tongue over her lips. "Not at all like the mealy berries you can't eat over at Martin's."

"Don't tell me that." Tom went back to foraging. "Tell him."

"Damn you." Her voice was low and soft as the creek flow.

"Seriously. He listens to you. Maybe you could get him to plant native berries in place of those silly cypress. And your lawn over there—"

"Martin's lawn."

"Whoever's. It's got no value. It's just useless and thirsty."

She picked at the berries. "You know, Martin mentioned your time in Las Vegas."

"What about it?"

"Just that you weren't with your wife there. That you might as well be divorced."

"Huh." Tom didn't speak for a minute, then said, "Well, tell him to leave the spring alone. The raccoons and deer and lion need it."

"Lion?"

She reached a cool hand behind his neck and pulled him in for a kiss. It started out soft but turned urgent and hard. After a minute he stood back and led her without touching into his parents' house. He wasn't sure she would follow, but she did. Inside, he turned to her with a freedom he had never felt within view of Martin's upstairs windows. They spent the day indoors, under the Hudson Bay blanket on the hide-a-bed. Out of her jeans, she was plumper than he'd imagined, with flesh he found ripe and delicious. In his arms, under him, she had a wild, abandoned look in her eyes. Throughout all their loving—embrace, union, release—he studied her changing face. He stayed watchful, a lens he believed caught his own lovemaking and her liberation.

. . .

Martin's return coincided with a bout of early winter rains. After Tom's night with Trudy, he drank late-morning coffee at his kitchen window, watching for Martin's big Lexus. When the sleek sedan did arrive, slipping out of the wet storm into the garage next to Trudy's Volkswagen, Tom imagined that Martin or Trudy or both would show up at his front door, demanding or giving some kind of confession.

Neither showed. Rain soaked everything in Tom's backyard, from the thick-branched bigleaf maple to the delicate snowberry. Puddles grew into ponds on dirt footpaths as rain sluiced to earth. In a daze, Tom startled when the phone rang in the mid afternoon. He jumped to pick up.

It was his parents' realtor. "The neighbor next door wants the house. Do you know Martin Banks? He said he knows you. He's buying it for his girlfriend." The papers were all in order, already signed and awaiting countersignature. Tom's throat tightened.

"By the way," said the realtor, "the only thing Mr. Banks didn't approve was the Native Flora and Fauna clause. He wants to replace the garden."

Tom managed to say he'd think about it, but after he hung up his anger grew. Throwing on a raincoat, pulling out his father's big black umbrella, he hurried down the front path. The rain fell in torrents. He rushed toward Martin's yard, reached the front walkway, and—kept going.

Following the creek to the hills, he started out on sidewalks, then climbed down into the channels. He closed the umbrella and tucked it under his arm, the green overstory of redwood, oak, and fir a shield above him. Among wet fern, tree bark, and earth, he spent a good hour following a lone pileated woodpecker along the creek. Where the male bird crossed to the other bank, Tom hopped boulders to cross, too. He stopped to rest when the woodpecker paused, listening as it pummeled the bark of a Doug-fir or bay before moving on.

After the woodpecker lost him in a line of redwood trees, and the day's light dulled, Tom headed back downstream. He felt a satisfied exhaustion from wandering. Who needed a native plant clause? There were woods right up the street. He would call the realtor, set up a time to sign.

Moments after arriving home and getting out of his wet clothes, wearing only a towel around his waist, he heard tapping at the front door. He swung it open.

"Trudy?" He was met by a burst of yapping: a small, white dog strained at a red leash held by a grim-faced Martin in a trench coat and tweed rainhat.

Tom forced a grin. "Hey! Is that . . . ?"

"Pommie. The Pets Ahoy people found him."

Scowling at Tom's bare chest and legs, Martin tossed a manila envelope at his feet. His little dog growled, then trotted alongside as he hustled away without a word, his trench coat collar pulled up, his shoulders hunched.

Tom retrieved the envelope, slid it onto the kitchen counter, and stood back from it. He paced, keeping his distance, until at last he reached for the envelope and broke the seal. Inside were two glossy, eight-by-ten photographs. At first he couldn't make them out: even with an obviously expert use of light, the shots had come out dark. Taken today during the rainstorm, he supposed. As he stared, he recognized human shapes framed by the culvert under Martin's driveway.

In the first picture, a tall, rough-looking man held a rifle. It was a 30-06, a caliber Tom knew from his hunting days. He'd never used a weapon with a silencer, though, as this one had—a canister as long as Tom's garden trowel. The hunter wore an Indiana Jones style fedora and camouflage jacket. At his feet lay an animal as big as a man, soft edged, and limp. The creek, swollen a bit from the rains, braided between the fallen beast and the hunter's rubber boots.

In a second photograph, Martin stood with tan cheeks and a white-toothed, thin-lipped smile beside the hunter, now squatting and holding the animal by the neck. Stretched to afford a full view, the prey had pointed cat ears, long tail, and shaggy underbelly. Its wide paws more than six inches across rested in curls, the authority gone from them.

Tom sunk to his knees on the shaggy carpet in the living room. He'd never broken down after Sue left, or when they had divided up goods from their marriage, or even when his parents had passed. But now he sobbed on the floor, photo beside him, his belly hurting as if he'd been punched.

. . .

In the backyard the next morning, Tom walked the paths in his folks' garden. The rain had paused. He felt empty, poured out. It had taken him most of the night, but he'd thought things through. He'd also packed his bags and done a final cleaning of the house. In the light of day, he carried two nine-by-twelve manila envelopes under one arm while he surveyed the manzanita borders—all of which he had pruned over the past weeks. The toyons and madrones, clear of dead branches, looked natural but cared for. It was the work he had come to do. The house and garden would show well now.

He didn't peek at Martin's house, but in his peripheral vision he saw a light come on upstairs. Perhaps a bathroom, off a master suite Martin shared with Trudy? Tom didn't know. He had never been inside, nor did he figure he'd ever go there now. After a moment, he couldn't stop himself looking, and he made out a silhouette framed by bright fluorescence. Too small a shape to be Martin's. He could call up to Trudy, but the window was closed. Was she humming to herself? Or looking in the mirror into animal eyes? He kept staring until the light clicked off as suddenly as it had come on.

Just as well—he didn't know what he would say if she were to open a window. Although, come to think of it, he could mention that his folks' house was still for sale. He planned to stop by the realtor's office on his way out of town. He would keep the place listed—another buyer would approve the Native Flora and Fauna clause. No reason to jump at the first offer. There was no hurry now, after all.

He strolled to the creekbank. The flow had risen higher and muddy from the rain, swelling enough to cover the hunter's tracks. The streambed would show no trace of what had happened in Martin's culvert. As Tom stood listening to the rush of current, he fingered the envelopes. The first held three of his point-and-shoot pictures: one of the lion track with time and date stamp; two of a glorious, happy Trudy up on Martin's roof, the sun in her hair.

The light came on again upstairs at Martin's. Tom held his breath. It was Trudy. Through the window, from the distance he'd advised her to keep from the creek, she met his gaze. There was something new about her expression. Anger? No, something else. Resignation? He couldn't be sure from that far away. She slammed the window but not before Tom caught the snapping bark of the Pomeranian from somewhere in the house.

Fine. He would post the envelopes with his photos within the hour. Martin and Trudy would receive the first one the next day. The second envelope, addressed to Brad, the Fish and Game warden, held the two hunting photos Martin had handed him. Tom had marked them with the Banks name and phone number. Trudy had done a beautiful job of documenting the demise of the lion, and Brad would want to know—all Tom had to do was pass on the information. He had kept copies of everything, to remind himself to follow up sometime after he'd wandered back up the coast.

His universe of big trees and flowing streams might be shrinking, but he'd still go there. It was still home.

Steelies

· · ·

No one listened when I warned about the water. The valley people, I mean. They always gave me the same empty looks, like nothing I said was new or true, and these mindless nods, no better than bobble-headed dolls. Like, "We're not about to stop pumping out of the creeks, so give it a rest, fish lady." That's what they called me—fish lady—and worse, probably, because I told them that sucking up water doesn't drain just the streambeds. You stand to lose everything: first the summer pools, then the wet river cobbles and wells, then the last, mighty fish named for the silver-blue dress they put on to spawn.

But why take my word for it? Anyone could follow me and see for himself. Brad was the only one who did, the only one who said he'd be there and then made sure he showed up. He asked to tour the creeks with me as part of his job for Fish and Game. I agreed, thinking he might be able to do something about all the hoses sucking water from the summer pools like straws.

When I first met Brad at the Fuller Creek confluence, an alarm went off in me. He was standing on the bank upstream of the cement plant, questioning homeless men under the MLK Jr. Avenue Bridge. He wore a tan uniform and a cap that I later learned covered a shaved head. His warden's badge caught the sun. He looked official, making notes. As I drove up, all I could think was he'd better not run those guys off—they make some of the best fish sightings in the valley from their streamside camp.

When I walked within earshot, I heard Jerry, the tall, gray-haired camp leader, filling Brad in about the flooding earlier in the season. Three days of solid rains back in April had swollen the creeks into muddy messes. Jerry and crew had been forced to move their furniture up the bank to keep it dry. While doing so Jerry noticed the backs of steelhead swimming upstream through the high water. Now the creek had fallen again and their couch was back at streamside, missing two of its three cushions. Curtis and Stoner, Jerry's two regular sidekicks, lay propped on elbows in the dirt just above the high-water mark, half-covered in sleeping bags. They all called me "fish lady," too, but in a nice way I didn't mind.

Brad asked Jerry if he'd ever seen any landowners siphoning the creek. Jerry pointed his thumb at me. "Ask R.J. She knows." Brad closed the cover on his metal clipboard and, for the first time, gave me his full attention. He looked me over head to toe—thinking who knows what—and I squirmed as I did in the presence of an official. And a handsome one, too, around my age. He took in my rubber boots, my notebook and pen, and my long, silver hair—it been gray and getting grayer since I was twenty-two. He didn't hesitate. He invited me to his state truck for a bottle of spring water.

Back in the Fish and Game six-pack, the first breeze of the afternoon crept through Brad's lowered windows. He poured cool water into my canteen. "You've seen spawners in the watershed, the males and females?"

I nodded.

"Even digging their redds? Actually nesting?"

"Of course." Surely he knew the fish were still here. The doe prepares the gravels, and the buck guards her, ready to release milt over her eggs. Just like in the textbooks. Usually the buck is battling the stray rainbows—young punks, you could say—who try to be first to the female. While the males fight to claim the streambed, the doe twirls, really graceful, as if she were born to dance. An acrobat.

Brad's eyes shone. "How about taking me to their spawning sites sometime?"

An electric current ran through me, but I don't think it showed. He didn't ask me about the hoses and water withdrawals, as Jerry had suggested, which I admit gave me pause. Maybe he didn't care about the siphoning at all; maybe he was all about the fish.

Early evening I returned home to a message on my phone machine from a local poet. He read a few lines from Rilke that ended with, "Within yourself, you one-time-child, within yourself." That's all I caught of it. "R.J., I hope you'll consider saying yes this time. Do call back." I erased the message.

The classical hour played on the radio as I typed up the day's notes. I hadn't seen any steelhead, but they're good at hiding. I had started my tracking up at Fox Creek, where the pools swirl in bedrock under the redwoods. The streams at the top of the watershed run cool and clear, dark in the shadows, light in the sun. Swallows wheel down from over the treetops, chasing some hatch or other, caddis flies mostly. And the creeks sometimes hold a lot of baby steelhead, or fry as they're called, with oval parr marks on their sides that look like flattened water beetles. Those tiny fish, just starting life, are the ones I call *steelies*. They're the creatures the valley philistines say are "small enough to live in a puddle, so what's the big deal, fish lady?"

Whenever I make notes about the headwaters, I follow the main stream down the valley, past vineyards, past the dairies. Everywhere a tributary enters, like Miwok or Orchard or Lincoln, I stop to look for fish, to find which creeks they run in. And I record what I see, like: "Two spawners holding in riffle on Embrazos Creek. Good shelter, gravel clean. Half-hour mating dance. No eggs yet."

In the south, where I end my route every afternoon, the creeks are warm and murky. The trash fish—pikeminnows and such—sit around waiting to lunch on the second-year steelhead on their way out to sea. The pikeminnows are native, too, but I find them heinous. They're nothing like the high-minded steelies, who want their water clear and cold on a summer day. Their epic journey to sea, followed by their return to find clean mating gravels, strikes me as the height of love.

As I worked at my desk, Mahler's Symphony No. 4 came on. I stopped to focus on the music while it took forever to climax. The strings drew out the melody while the woodwinds pranced to the rhythm of sleigh bells in the percussion section. Sleigh bells! You don't hear those every day.

I wandered to my open window. In the forest behind my backyard, the oaks had leafed out. The buckeyes, too, were green and tender, with flowered spikes in bloom: creamy blossoms, waving in the breeze, limber and reaching up. The music built, with the horns coming in like streams feeding a river, until everything flowed together and I couldn't tell one instrument from the next.

I returned to my notes, but the music held me. It crescendoed, a flood of music with all the instruments pouring out in unison. They ended in three abrupt, ear-pounding chords. Then it was over. The words on the page blurred through the tears in my eyes. Again the window drew me—in the evening light, the buckeye blooms glowed and swayed. I thought of Brad in his tan pants and how they might look if his own spike were stiff in them. My God. Here I had just met him, and I was already having thoughts of pollination. Maybe I'd been alone too long and dwelling too much on the mating of fish.

That was just it. What I needed was a man who could fill the creek to overflowing. I hadn't tried partnering since my husband, Bob, had followed his dream to Maui to manage a dive shop. He'd wanted me to go with him, but I didn't think I could abandon the creeks.

But why not, really? What good was I doing touring around the watershed spying on steelies like some kind of fish pervert?

That night I lay in bed with the sweats, my body hot as a frying potato, my skin wet and slick. My doctor had said that the night heat comes from the change of life, which wasn't far off for me. Whatever, but those flashes reminded me of steelhead baking on summer cobbles out in the streams. The juveniles would be there soon, returning to the drawn-down creeks, stranded with not-enough water. And I'd be here, lying above the sheets, covered in way too much.

•　•　•

Brad didn't get back in touch for nine months. Right away I'd been desperate for his help with the fish, but June turned to July without a word, then summer to autumn. Some steelies had taken shelter in the cool pools up in the headwaters, but many more were not so fortunate. There was nothing to do but record the numbers dying in the hot streambeds and pray Brad would help bring the power of the government to bear on their life-and-death struggles. When he didn't show, I despaired over the losses. I even phoned Bob in Lahaina and sobbed, and he begged me to come join him at the dive shop. He'd been lonely over there, he said, and even the fish had mates, didn't they?

Before I could find the right plane ticket on Maui Air, though, winter came on, wet and exciting. Mature fish were turning up like lost coins throughout the watershed. I stopped searching for air passage. Driving my route took a turn for the best as I counted adults who'd arrived to start a new batch of steelies. Valiant fish—like bees reclaiming a cleaned-out hive. My heart raced in their presence.

The big storms passed. The new year came. One clear February morning, I sat on a boulder near Esperanza Creek, making notes. A pair of mallards dabbled in an eddy beyond the willows, and the stream sang over its bed. Blackberry and poison oak were just getting their new, fresh green leaves. Only an occasional car passed on the old highway bridge nearby. Sitting by the pool with my notebook, I waited as still as a heron.

Up above, high clouds swam in a pale blue sky. Their reflections brightened the water, hypnotizing me with their slow shimmer. After some time I got the sense someone was watching me, and I looked up to see Brad at the top of the bank, the sun glowing behind his cap.

"I saw your car," he said.

It had been months since I'd thought of him in botanical terms, but I still couldn't meet his eyes as he climbed down the bank. He sat not ten feet away, and I kept my gaze on the water. He knew to be quiet as we kept watch for the fish. After a while of sitting by the stream, hearing it sieve through the shallows, we whispered a bit of conversation. Brad said he'd been back in Alaska, his home base. He'd grown up fishing for salmon, then had followed various jobs until he ended up here. "It was good to be home," he said. "Though it was colder than a polar bear's ass. But the fish there! Still as big as baby dolphins." He showed me their size with his hands. "Not many steelhead, though."

As if called up, two steelhead edged into the pool right before us. Not the size of Brad's Alaskan salmon, but still more than a foot-and-a-half, tip to tail. First they were just a ripple, then rising sleek bodies. Then they were a couple dancing like foam in an eddy.

"It's a pair!" he said. "Two adults."

Moving together, they slid up the rumpled water of the riffle. In the flow from a higher pool, they stopped and hovered like hawks. Brad and I got a good look. The doe, a few inches shorter than the buck, lay low while he drifted above her. He guarded her left, then quivered back to her right, more than once blowing back in the current. When that happened he had to push back stronger to regain his place at her side.

Just as I wondered where the combative young trout were, two six-inch male rainbows darted in from upstream.

"There are the jacks!" Brad pointed.

They greased in past the buck like sports cars slipping by a long-haul semi. Working into place beside the doe, they stayed for only three seconds before the buck fought them off. When the current separated him and his intended, he gathered his wits and struggled back to her. Over and over, the jacks darted in; over and over the buck pushed in and edged them out.

"It's got to be his milt," Brad said. "Or nobody's."

The drama played on for the next ten minutes. The doe held her place as the buck acted as sentry to her carnal treasure. All of this happened in three square feet of streambed—one little patch of gravel and cobble and life-giving fluid. Life and death, DNA and evolution, all right there before us. I couldn't breathe for the passion of the courtship before us.

Just as I thought the jacks might whip the buck, they gave up and drifted away. "Now it's time," I said.

In a move resembling the dead zinging back to life, the female rolled over, her body a long blade sweeping the current. She used water as a tool to shift a handful of gravel in the creek.

"She's digging in!" Brad raised himself from his haunches. Without thinking, he cast a shadow over the pool.

The doe and buck steelhead fled, their downstream exit ruffling the water in flexing lines.

"No!" Brad held his head in his hands.

"'No' is right," boomed a voice. "Shouldn't scare them like that, son."

Brad and I both startled. Across the creek stood Harry Cabot-Boon, a big-bodied vintner who grew grapes on a thousand acres over there. He rested big hands on his massive hips. His Red Wing boots and blue jeans with checked dress shirt signaled loud and clear that he worked in both field and office.

"Sorry." He grinned. "Didn't mean to frighten you."

Bending to my pen and notebook, I wished I could disappear. Cabot-Boon was never pleasant out on the creek. In town he wasn't bad; but outdoors, he turned downright rude. As if he owned the whole valley and we who did not violated some code. Brad made conversation with him, though, friendly and joking across the water. While they spoke I scrawled notes about the spawning ritual we'd just witnessed.

"Hey, Harry," Brad called to him. "R.J. says the creek's been going dry here. Seen anybody drawing water out of these pools?"

Cabot-Boon snorted. "Oh, hell, we all know that's against the law."

Brad swung a look toward me as Cabot-Boon peered at his watch.

"Sorry" the vintner said. "Love to chat but got to run. Let's pick this up again soon."

After Cabot-Boon had left with his signature stealth, the fish returned. The female resumed her dance while the male held there, tail fanning, still waiting for the completion he'd anticipated all his life. Once the doe finished making her nest and squeezed out her eggs in a soft mass, the buck released his pent-up stream in a milky cloud. His face was turned away from me, but I knew how he'd look: lips apart in a silent shriek, body trembling, eyes stunned wide open.

As the male let loose, Brad leaned into me. He circled my waist with his arms, pressing his mouth to the back of my neck. His mouth felt like a blaze on my skin. I didn't fight him, but I checked to make sure Cabot-Boon was really gone. To my relief there was nothing over there but trees and blackberry. I let my weight relax against Brad, free falling.

. . .

After that Brad and I didn't miss touring the watershed together once a week. We saw everything—adult steelhead in the pools on Radigan Creek, squawfish lurking like piranha below Parson Dam, mitten crabs scuttling on old bridge piers at Agua Fria Road. We shared long lunches beside pretty pools at the Esperanza-Fox confluence and detoured a few times to the waterfall where nursery fish would gather in summer. I showed him the sucking hoses and talked about the deaths by drying. He said there was nothing we could do. I argued that we had to do something.

Then, on a day in April with only a hint of heat, we circled back to the spawning site near the old highway bridge. We saw the fry, brand new, thick as ants on a mound. They were steelies, not even two inches long. Brad scooped one up with his hands, the little thing tender and see-through on the lifeline of his palm. The baby fish gasped as water ran out between Brad's fingers.

My heart thumped hard. "Put it back!"

He lowered his hand to the stream, murmuring. The steelie floated rigid in the shallow water above his skin.

Brad looked crushed. "But it was just a few seconds."

"Those tiny things can't make it for long out here." My breath came out jagged. I opened my notebook and clicked my pen to record the death.

"You can't write about it!" His eyes were wide. "I just broke the law. Hell, even if it had lived it could be considered a take."

"A take?"

"You know! A capture. Under the Endangered Species Act." He swept the steelie out to the sand. Then he walked to his truck without saying goodbye.

The little fish lay at my feet. Already sunken, it was becoming part of the sandy earth. I could wait and make a note of its fate—whether a heron got it for lunch or a raccoon discovered it. Or whether it would just keep drying out and turn to dust. The sight of it hurt me somewhere under my sternum. I gathered my gear and headed for my car.

◆　◆　◆

Brad stayed away again and, in a fit of loneliness, I consented to dinner out with the local poet. We spent one long, dull evening where he regaled me with quotations. "So romantic," he said, "that you're playing hard to get. 'To wait Eternity—is short—If Love's reward the end'—Emily Dickinson." He lifted his glass of chardonnay. As he dropped me off at home, he said, "'The course of true love never did run smooth'—Shakespeare, *A Midsummer Night's Dream*." He called me later to say what a fine time he'd had, and I let the machine take it. Later I dialed Bob in Lahaina but hung up before the connection clicked through.

The days brought more sun, more drying. Spring left in a hurry—a few rainstorms passed, and summer followed with no warning. The pools were dropping, the fish crowding like refugees into what water remained. They had grown a few inches longer and stronger in their bodies, like seedlings that get to be trees. They needed space; they needed water. At the spawning site near the old highway bridge, a mass of them had gathered in a four-inch-deep pool. At the rate things were going, they would be stranded in a week.

The sun bore down. Cars hummed by at intervals. A black phoebe flitted between the creek and a cottonwood, going after insects. I studied the pool and listened to traffic noise until I was numb. Then, unable to think straight, I left. A few miles down the road, I realized I had forgotten my notebook. Returning to park in my usual spot, I slipped toward the creekbank where the phoebe was still trying for bugs. My notebook lay near the water, which had dropped two inches in the time I'd been away. That's when I saw it: a wet ring, damp soil rimming the top of the pool that had been higher not fifteen minutes before. The fish were crammed into the remaining water, no flow going in or out. They looked like a mass of worms, writhing, struggling to get wet enough to breathe.

Someone had to be pumping water from the creek. In the dry season, in the middle of the day. Maybe they had rights, and maybe they had been grandfathered in before the new rules, but they were killing the commons.

What to do? I couldn't get my net and bucket and evacuate the fish—moving endangered species was a crime. Brad had been clear that I could be accused of a take. I'd read up on it in the days since: one farmer in the south valley was facing jail time for transferring rare red-legged frogs from one pond to another on his own property. He'd already paid ten grand in fines.

I ran upstream, hopping rocks. Most of the creekbed was dry, but mud in remnant pools sucked at my shoes each time I landed. Blackberry vines snagged and ripped my shirt as I pushed past. Willow limbs whipped my skin, leaving catkin bits on my arms. A low-hanging branch knocked off my hat, but I didn't stop for it. Up ahead was the machine noise and gurgle of air and water I was seeking. In a moment I almost stumbled on a length of black hose. Three inches in diameter and dozens of feet long, it could have been a snake—it meandered from the creek and back into brush farther up the bank. I yanked on the hose but couldn't budge it. I tried to rip it open, but it was too strong. At last I picked up a piece of dark glassy rock with sharp edges—obsidian, I guess—and attacked it. I pounded, pounded, and gashed until I made a big hole. Then I continued hacking until I tore off three feet to take as evidence. The pump rumbled and inhaled air.

Hose in hand, I ran to my car and started driving. I had no plan. I had to force myself to pause at the stop signs. If the pools could drop two inches in fifteen minutes, what would be left by the end of the day? Not enough water to cover a single pair of gills. Maybe there would be suffocation by the dozens. By the hundreds.

I found myself heading for the government offices at city hall. As I parked and hurried inside, I missed seeing Brad's truck five spaces away. Bursting through the front door to the offices, hose in hand, I realized too late that I'd pushed in on some kind of meeting. People sat facing the front of the room, and they turned to look at me. There were dairy farmers, vintners, men from the local water board—all well groomed and pressed in business clothes. Harry Cabot-Boon was there, stuffed into the same grower costume, surrounded by a group of buddies. There was the president of the golf club, the superintendent of parks and recreation, a few of the city maintenance guys. The mayor. Only one other woman was in sight, typing up minutes in the front of the room.

Brad stood behind the podium, frozen mid-sentence.

"Hello, R.J.," he said, his first words to me in weeks. "Have a seat."

"I can't. The fish are out of water!"

I knew my pants were hemmed in mud, my shirt snagged by blackberry thorns. No doubt my face showed tear streaks and my hair hung in a tangle.

There were murmurs all around. Brad put up his hands to quiet the crowd.

"Yes," he said, so all could hear. "That's why we're meeting. To work on an MOU for Aquatic Species."

I stared at him, not comprehending.

"A Memorandum of Understanding," he added. "It will be signed and active in six months."

"Six months!" I held up the section of black hose, the proof of water thievery he had been seeking when we first met. "I found this in the creek. Just now. Pumping it dry."

Brad kept his expression neutral. He held papers in a sheaf above the podium.

"Brad," I said. "They'll die if we don't move them."

"They may die if we do." Droplets of sweat rimmed his eyebrows.

A voice boomed from the audience. It was Cabot-Boon. "You know," he said. "Moving those endangered fish is against the law."

"Right." Brad nodded. "Moving them is considered take."

I turned to the plump, well-watered bodies squeezed into chairs. My cheeks were flushed, I knew. Forcing myself to meet their eyes, I held up the length of hose.

"Isn't this a take, too?" I faced Brad. "Isn't it? Taking water that kills the fish?"

"This yours?" I looked at Cabot-Boon.

"Or yours?" I asked another grower I had seen in the papers, a millionaire wine heir barely out of college. He sat with his mouth hanging open, like he'd never signed up for such a life, and shifted his gaze to the floor. All the growers did, one by one. No one owned the hoses. The room grew as hushed as the city morgue.

In a moment Brad took my arm as if I were sick or injured and guided me toward the door. I pulled away. He latched onto me again, harder this time, so I let him lead me down the aisle. There was silence around us, until we reached the last row.

Then someone behind us hissed. "Fish lady."

I whipped around. They all kept their eyes away. No one seemed to have spoken.

Brad released me when we reached my car. "Don't mess things up, R.J. I'm serious."

He abandoned me there—hose in my hand. He left me alone, dirty, and afraid, and he returned to the meeting with the men in chairs.

. . .

That night the moon waxed full, and I had the classical hour on again. This time I lay in bed on top of my sheets, eyes open, feeling the weight of the heat. Even with the windows open, my bedroom was as stuffy as a schoolhouse. The sweats hadn't yet hit, and I prayed they wouldn't. My radio played Brahms, whose name always makes me think of lullabies, but this was a rowdy piece: the "Academic Festival Overture." All the strings buzzed away, so busy, working toward a peak. As I lay there listening to the action, I felt nowhere near slumber. The humming of the strings sounded more like insects than music.

I thought of cicadas, then the willows they inhabit, then the creek they border. My mind went to the fish again. Canaries in the coal mine. If they dried up and spirited away, we wouldn't be far behind. We lived in the same web of water, the same strand of survival. As I pondered it, a call came in to my answering machine.

"R.J., it's Bob. Great news! I've met someone in Lahaina, she's really special. Please pick up, I know you're there . . . "

Great. Another escape valve gone. I tuned out the rest of his message as I focused on the orchestra, still building.

In a rush, after taking forever to get there, the piece reached a thrilling climax. As the music swelled, I felt my body rise with it, something inside me that surfaced like a trout to a fly. Then it was over in sixty seconds. Sixty seconds! The moment came and went that fast.

Enough. I got up, pulled on my clothes, and slipped out of the house. Heading for my car, I picked up gear from my shed: dip net, bucket, water shoes, headlamp. The moon had climbed high overhead. I could have driven with my headlights off, it was so bright. But I didn't. I kept on as normally as possible to the old highway bridge and the spawning site. Not wanting to be seen from any of the country homes, I continued past my usual pull-off. I didn't even turn my head to look and didn't slow down until I'd made it around the corner and into an ash grove. Then, switching off my lights, I left my car well hidden. There was no traffic. No one would see me walk to the bridge and climb down to the pool.

By the light of the moon, I could tell that the creek had risen again. At the water's edge, I switched on my headlamp. In the glow I could see steelies who hadn't made it: a half dozen floated belly-up on the water's surface. Others lay dead at the edge of the pool. I picked one up—it was wrinkled, like it'd been freeze-dried, its eyeballs crumpled in a lifeless stare. My own eyes blurred with tears. My heart bounded like something made of rubber in my chest.

I scooped dead steelies out of the water. Then I dipped the net back in for live ones. After several tries—close calls, I was still getting the knack—I heard a vehicle coming, creeping down the road. Clicking off my headlamp, I drew my gear under the bridge. A truck driving with only its parking lights on passed above me and parked. The lights switched off. A boot crunched on gravel.

I listened and waited. My heart still pumped like a machine you can't turn off. A flashlight beam played on the creek bank, then the gravel bar, then the water. I glanced at the pool and . . . my bucket! White as a July moon, it was still sitting at the rim of the pool near the dead steelies. I withdrew farther into the shadow under the bridge.

The flashlight beam traveled from the pool to the bucket, passed it, then returned to the bucket and snapped off. There was the sound of footsteps, the sight of boots, a pair of jeans, and a torso in a light jacket. A shaved head shone in the moonlight. Brad, out of uniform. He picked up the bucket and peered around. He stood a minute, looking and listening.

He switched his flashlight back on, studying the pool, his face reflected in the glow off the water. Many moments passed, as if he were counting, thinking. Then he held the flashlight in his teeth and bent close to the water. He dipped in with the bucket, lighting his way with the wandering beam. I saw him try and miss, try and miss. He cursed. They were getting away from him.

I moved out of hiding and switched on my headlamp. "That won't work."

Brad dropped the bucket. "Christ!"

"You're going to need this instead." I extended my dip net to him.

He came closer and stood face to face with me. Letting out a long breath, he touched my cheek. "I'm sorry, R.J. I've been a total dick."

I felt the crazy beating of my heart settle down. "And I've been a . . . fish lady."

He chuckled. "Come on. We can move them to a better pool upstream."

I nodded, and we got to work. We found we didn't need our lights, the moon was bright enough. We caught steelie after steelie, more than you might've thought were there just by looking. It was a cinch—Brad used the dip net as I held a bucket of water, and we transferred the little fish upstream to a deep pool under a full canopy of oak and bay. As we worked together, we made sure no steelie was out of the water for more than a few seconds. Longer than that, we both knew, would be too long.

The Red Skiff

. . .

George Nelson sensed he would die young; the darkness was in his blood. His mother and two sisters watched him with vigilance, as eagles watch the river. The plea never left the women's eyes, the prayer that he not follow the path taken by his father and brothers. His mother could have come straight out and begged, but she didn't. Instead her hope for his long life emanated in unspoken words, her wishes for his safety woven in the air. He answered her concerns with, "I'm not going down like the others. I'm careful in the skiff—I don't drink, I follow the rules, I know the tides."

She and George's sisters relaxed at his reassurance, but only for a short while. He knew their fear lingered, and why shouldn't it? In his family, bad luck had a way of overriding caution and hope.

His father, George Sr., had described their outlook in a dark vision. "Just when I think our fortunes will turn around, I see blackness, like the deepest part of the ocean. Next thing you know, lady luck turns her back. And there's no getting past her."

Of course George Sr. had been over in the saloon prior to coming up with that one, with drink shading his mood as nothing else could. Two days later, he vanished from the family troller, the *Ocean Eagle,* when a windstorm blew up the inlet and battered the boat as he tried to secure its mooring. His body washed to shore near the ferry loading ramp, where it was spotted by a tourist. George's mother and sister sobbed for days, while George maintained a silent bafflement over his father's inability to save himself so close to shore.

One year and a day later, George's three older brothers died at sea. He had been too sick to fish that day. Bad clam chowder from the Shiner Diner had emptied him out, so he wasn't there when David, Ben, and Roy, all demigods to George, were lost together in a squall that blew up out of a calm morning. The troller, *Ocean Eagle,* went down with them.

George woke the next morning to learn he'd lost half his remaining family overnight and, in the many months since, he refused to crew on any boat. He would only leave shore in his red skiff.

He wore the Nelson family traits as he wore the name: pale hair, sturdy build, sharp blue eyes always searching. The apartment where he lived near his mother and sisters was as bright as possible for a coastal hometown that got ninety inches of rainfall a year and forty inches of snow. When his inherited gloom or the weather didn't oppress him, breezes through the spruce and alder on shore carried hope. He knew the salmon spawning, dying, and stinking up the rivers outside of town were a good sign—it meant the fish were still out there if he could just get to them. On his darker days, George felt a blackness darker than a raven's eyes after sundown—an inky hopelessness that matched his father's vision of the bottomless sea.

George had learned to troll from George Sr. He took pride in hooking and cleaning chinook, coho, and chum salmon and treated each one with respect. He knew how to keep the fish fresh and unbruised before shipping. Trolling topped his list of things worth doing, but it was impossible without the *Eagle*. He and his brothers had struggled enough with the complex maze of licenses, season start and end dates, fishing limits, and area closures. No way George could do it himself—and losing the troller had sounded the death knell for the family business. The Nelsons hadn't been carrying insurance on the *Eagle* for two years, leaving George stranded when it sunk.

He did have a job, sort of. One day he had agreed to motor the Fish and Game warden around the inlet, and it had turned into a regular paying gig. George used his skiff, which still had its original red paint and the fifteen-horsepower Suzuki motor his father had bought to replace an ancient but powerful Merc. Though sturdy, the skiff was plagued by leaking floor seams, and George couldn't keep ahead of their continual loosening. He sealed them as often as he could stand to bring the boat out of the water, put it under tarps, and dry it to the extent the southeast Alaska weather allowed. Even flawed, the skiff came to be one piece of his world George could trust.

He suspected that the warden, Brad, could explore the inlet on his own. Brad had access to all kinds of boats at his job, and he was a smart guy with lots of friends. He had grown up in Alaska, too, then come back after fishing down south. He knew his way around motors and oars as most government employees didn't. His wife, R.J., was some sort of boater and steelhead expert, now studying salmon, and she came in the skiff, too. Those two seemed to prefer that George guide them rather than going on their own—that was obvious.

They asked discreet questions, but they couldn't hide their fascination with native wisdom. What ancient fishing customs did you pick up from growing up around here? Has your friend Calvin the totem carver shared anything about how salmon find their way home?

George returned polite but brief answers. He didn't want to lose the job, but asking him to speak for Calvin and the tribe turned a good day bad in a hurry. It was tough enough to have to make a living touring around with a couple from down south without being reminded of the old, lost ways he'd heard Calvin harp on again and again. He'd rather motor solo any day and forget the talk. Even when his father and brothers were alive, George would sometimes go alone in the skiff on his days off. He'd steal away to throw out single lines in No Way Bay and keep only solitude for company. That bay attracted few boaters, divided as it was from the inlet by a channel that filled with boat-eating whitewater when the tide hurried back out to sea.

•　•　•

Whenever George motored close to the downtown, he'd check to see if Calvin's workshop doors were open. If they were, George aimed for shore, docked the skiff, and walked the long block to visit the totem carver. George would sit on a tree-stump seat while Calvin labored over cedar poles, his long, carbon-black hair held back in a ponytail. Calvin was from farther southeast but had come to town at least a decade before. He'd converted a garage on the main street into a workshop open to the sidewalk, where he kept bistro stools and a coffee cart. Tools hung on a red-and-black pegboard behind him. When cruise ships arrived, or even the state ferries, he put out a sandwich sign inviting passersby to watch him cut and repaint wood.

Now Calvin was rehabilitating a totem that had been cracking, as poles did over time. He had removed the bolts and nails used in earlier attempts to hold the wood together. "Allowing it to split helps relieve pressure in the cedar. It's what the tree wants to do."

Calvin couldn't always give George his full attention, as the visitors' questions took precedence. Then George sat listening, smoking hand-rolled tobacco. He enjoyed the carver's storytelling and full, deep voice. Today Calvin was speaking to a handful of tourists who had arrived on a small-boat shuttle from the latest cruise ship that was moored, as many-windowed and imposing as a small city, just offshore.

"This is the Russian lord." Calvin pointed to the squat human figure at the top of the pole. "Then farther down here we have the chief from the Raven clan."

Other emblems—Bear, Frog, and Eagle—sat above and below the chief, although none dwarfed him. All were receiving new paint. Now Calvin was refreshing the whiteness of Eagle's head.

"How does the Russian get to be top guy on the totem pole?" asked a big man wearing a *Red Sox* ballcap. His poncho, one of the ship's white PVC handouts sprinkled with tiny blue *Alaska!* logos, hung just past his crotch.

A woman with frizzed red hair groaned. "Peter, don't."

Calvin only smiled. "Joining different cultures in the art form represents well-being among nations. It's a peace pole."

"Well said!" Peter applauded, a bit too loud to George's ears.

George wanted to add, "Yeah, and the dude farther down the pole is the baddest-ass," but he stayed silent.

After the visitors left, George rose from the stump-seat to view the progress on Eagle. He waited before asking, "How can you say that crap about peace between nations?"

"Crap?" Calvin straightened up, reaching his full height. He was a head taller than George, and now his eyes were wide. "Even my Grandfather Jacob wouldn't call it that."

"I thought all your grandfathers were dead."

Calvin set aside his paintbrush. "They are. But before they crossed over, they showed me how to go on. Especially Jacob. I mean, here was a man who'd lost everything. His only son—my father—killed trying to break up a bar fight in Juneau. His wife—my grandmother—dead of tuberculosis at forty. He took each blow like a wound gained in battle."

"But you told me Grandfather Jacob lost his will to carve."

"He did, after a bad deal with a trader." Calvin shook his head. "Grandfather's last piece, a Killer Whale bowl, took him a year to make, starting with the cutting of the wood. He held all the ceremonies, everything done the old way. After it was finished, he consigned it with a trader who sold it in a matter of days. It was masterful."

"And?"

"And the trader never made good on the sale, never paid him his commission. Oh, Jacob did his best, reported it where he was supposed to, went in person to the borough. But no one could help him, or so they said. He never did another piece."

"I'm a white guy, so I can say this. We suck."

"It's not just you. It's human nature." Calvin shook his head and went back to painting. "I thought I could live in both worlds—here and on Taan, or so-called Prince of Wales Island. But I don't go there now. Most of the villages have been raided. Stuff was carried off, even the burial boxes."

"White raiders?"

"Yes, and rival family groups. Pretty much anyone."

Calvin's face and voice revealed no bitterness. "My mother stays away from Taan, too. She lives in Ketchikan. You know that, I visit her sometimes. Thankfully I convinced Grandfather Jacob to teach me to carve. What I do helps keep my family alive."

George stared at his feet, wishing he were back in the skiff. If other visitors came, he would slip out before there was more talk. No one else wandered in, though, and he stayed at the shop until the mouth of the inlet glowed with midday sun.

"You going home for lunch, George?" Calvin asked. "Or should I ask Freda to add a plate to our table?"

George wanted to head up to No Way Bay while light still brightened the opposite shore.

"No thanks, Calvin. I'm going back to the skiff."

• • •

Gloom caught up with George as he motored from the dock. Calvin was lucky; he had tribal tradition as the overarching law keeping balance in his world. He didn't doubt his people; they shone like a beacon in his world. George Sr. had sung the praises of the indigenous ways that had reigned fishing before government regulations came along to replace them. Back then, the Nelsons had always earned more than enough from the sea to live on and sell at market. When greater restrictions came later, they pushed his family and most others he knew to the edge.

Wind had come up on the inlet. He hadn't checked the tide book, but he knew the falling sea would soon be sieving through rocks in the channel opening to the bay. Ebb tide was the most dangerous time there. He knew, because he'd been out before in dicey conditions—jockeying the skiff in the current like buck salmon fighting jacks, fully aware of how dangerous the ice-cold bay could be. He knew of plenty of prior accidents there: boats that had left shore in fair conditions, only to fight the swells when coming home. It wasn't intentional that he should tempt fate, he realized; it was just that the slate-gray rocks and flashing rapids of the channel drew him. Getting to No Way Bay, he usually felt the family gloom lift; something about water moving through rocks cleared the pervasive, crippling fog.

He thought of his mother's pleading eyes and waved them off with a swipe of his hand.

As he drove up the inlet, he brooded on everything lost and the things he couldn't do. Or have. Thousands of people stepped off the ships every day with more money than God. They paraded through town in designer hiking boots, carrying sacks of goods from boutique shops. He was well aware of how much wealth, good money that could buy a new troller, was being thrown at stuffed puffins and imitation fur-trader hats.

Twenty grand. That was what he needed to purchase a used boat. He laughed and heard anger in the sound. Might as well wish for a mansion in Cedar Heights, far from his own small apartment.

He kept the engine steady as he gripped the gunnel of the red skiff with his free hand. Autumn filled the air. So did the burnt-tire stench of pink salmon spawning and dying in Russian Creek. Light angled into spruce-green slopes ringing the inlet. Water splashed in the bottom of his boat. A few rivets were leaking. He felt his fury rise again over the money he needed, then remembered Calvin. He wished he had the carver's calm. He should have accepted the offer for lunch.

The tide had turned. A damp high-water ring showed at the sharp tree boundary at shore. Good. Falling tide. Conditions might be perfect for running the rapids by the time he motored into the channel. Out of habit he checked the straps on his lifejacket, chafed at its confinement, and unfastened it. He let it drop to the bottom of the boat. He remembered his father and brothers, how they had always worn lifejackets but had failed to survive anyway—as a humpback whale surfaced beside the skiff and shot mist twenty feet into the air.

"Christ!" George about fell off his seat.

He settled again, heart pounding, as the whale rolled down. Another one, much smaller, surfaced, too—once, twice, three times—forcing out a cloud and rush of air on each emergence. On the fourth rising, the small whale raised itself higher, showing more dorsal fin, then plunged deeper, displaying its young flukes as if they were new wings. The mother rose again, blowing a thunderous plume of salt water and waving her own shimmering, mature flukes before disappearing. George smiled, observed himself smiling, and scowled. He'd always heard you're not close to a whale unless you smell its primal, oceanic breath, but he could smell nothing. Even they were distant from him on this day.

"It doesn't matter," he muttered.

Reaching the rocky channel that led to the bay, George could see in a moment that the tide wasn't as low as he'd hoped. He cursed the ocean—and immediately regretted it. "It's my own fault," he admitted. "For not checking ahead." He called to the ocean, asking forgiveness. He was subject to superstition, he knew. His father had taught him that those who respected nature lived and died by it. Those who did not were on their own, neither aided nor fazed by their ignorance. A flatliner's life, in George's opinion.

A silver cabin cruiser entered the channel from the far end. It was a government rig, George guessed, although he couldn't yet make out an insignia. Radar rotated on a pole near the steering well. The cruiser rumbled toward him, then throttled down and drew within thirty feet of his skiff. It was Fish and Game. The captain cut the engine and called to him through a megaphone.

"Personal floatation devices are required."

Damn. It was Brad, in raingear, watch cap, and an orange lifejacket. He hadn't recognized George yet but did as he drifted closer. "Hey, George! Didn't see that was you. Here, let me lend you a PFD."

George smiled and shook his head. He picked up his own lifejacket, threaded his arms through it, and snapped the buckles. He shrugged and smiled bigger.

"Trying to get yourself killed?" Brad shook his finger in mock scolding. "It's getting bad in the channel. You should see the chop back there. Let's run back to town together."

George almost turned him down. But he remembered there would be a pole raising the next day, a ritual that Calvin had taken charge of, and everybody he knew would be there. Tomorrow he could slip back up to No Way Bay unnoticed.

"Sure," he said to Brad, feeling blackness press on him with an even greater weight.

.   .   .

The next day dawned an Eagle day. Damn. George knew it as soon as he woke to a clear sky and scanned the shore his window. Bald eagles perched on the posts near his skiff. Later in the morning, cormorants would claim those same spots, and by evening gulls would take them over and not budge for hours. But now there were four eagles—two standing motionless on the posts and two more that came and went. None were accomplishing much that George could see. They seemed to be resting, the way a cat does, saving energy for important work later.

Eagles inspired confusion in George. In the stories Calvin had told him, Eagle meant power. In those tales Eagle swept down from the mountains like Thunderbird, filled with great purpose. Calvin said you couldn't beat Thunderbird energy, it was top drawer. And the eagles George observed in real life spent most of their time picking over trash heaps. What did they have in common with the great, fierce Thunderbird?

His mother called on the land line, the only telephone George had anymore since the family cell phone plan had expired. "George," she whispered. "Your father and brothers are watching you today."

"What? From where?"

"Shh! Not so loud. You'll scare them off. Haven't you looked outside?"

"Mom, it's just pink salmon season. Eagles are everywhere."

"But four of them? Down by your boat? They know you're up to something."

"Not true. I'm up to almost nothing."

"I'll call Christine and Martha to go out fishing with you."

His sisters. "No, Mom, that won't help."

"Then go see Calvin. He called last night. He wants to know if you're coming to the Peace Pole raising this evening."

"He must've called to invite you. You're the one involved in the community council with him."

"The raising's at sundown. Everyone will be there, all the families, all the clans, all—"

"I'll go see Calvin." George hung up without hearing the rest.

He was aware of his own disrespect, cutting off his mother's speech. But the familiar feeling was descending. If he let it fall farther, he might use stronger words. Worse, it would paralyze him, and he would never get out of his apartment.

He tried to think. A pole raising meant there would be feasting. The New Potlatch, Calvin called it. New Potlatch meant everyone was invited, even tourists. Guests from all over would eat and laugh and drink like they belonged there or knew the meaning of the gathering. He looked at his socks, thinking about putting them on his feet. Several minutes passed. He wanted the troller back.

He checked his tide book. Out of habit his eyes went first to the symbol that ranked fishing conditions. It showed a big fish. Good out there today. Damn. Not long ago, he would've been gone already. His shoes would've been on his feet in seconds. He looked at the time for low tide—he'd have to hit the afternoon low since he'd missed the morning. Lowest tide at four twenty-one. Good. That was about the time everyone would be getting ready for the pole raising.

He would've stopped to see Calvin, as he'd told his mother, but the carver's doors were closed when George motored past. Just as well. He felt a strong urge to get to No Way Bay before the tide fell. Maybe he could drive up and cast a line out for salmon without having to see anybody. Brad wouldn't be patrolling the same waters a second day in a row. And there would be the thrill of rapids in the channel on his way home.

George kept his speed slow across the inlet. The sky looked as clear as fresh snowmelt, with a warm wind from the east. Too warm. Maybe it was the warming he had been warned would come even here: Calvin had said the whole world would slip so far out of balance that ice fields would thaw. Polar bears would mate with brown bears. Whales and other aquatic creatures would shift the season and distance of their migrations.

"How soon is that coming?" George had asked.

Calvin didn't know or wouldn't say. "It's something my grandfather told me, passed down from his father." All through the ages, warming had wiped out tribes that moved too far from their center. But the new warming would be worldwide, as if the Earth itself made heat like the sun and nothing in the universe could cool it.

George often forgot about the warming, but on a day like today, the breeze reminded him. Maybe it was too hot for a trip to No Way Bay. A melting wind among mountains lined with glaciers? The thought unnerved him as he aimed his skiff for the channel.

Nearing the opening in the wooded coastline, he felt his lifejacket confining him again. He undid the buckles and threw it onto the floor of the skiff, frowning as the orange vest fell in water that had seeped through the rivets. Even as he saw the material dampen and darken, he knew he was being foolish. With the shadow feeling still in him, though, he was powerless to change.

When he reached the bay, pink salmon surfaced all around and started him fishing. It wasn't warm there, he noticed, near the thick forest hemming the rock-lined shore. He hadn't brought a cooler, but he did have his knife. He cut cedar boughs that hung close to the water. They would hold his catch on the aluminum floor where it curved highest and stayed dry, far in the bow.

The day passed with ease as he sat with line out. Enjoying the sunlight and warmth of the breeze, which he forgot to abhor, he lost track of time. He felt lighter as the hours dissolved. Although he had left his license home, he knew his limit. When he reached it, he decided to motor back down the channel, cross the inlet, and continue into town to share his bounty at the pole raising. He hummed, thinking of how his mother and sisters would smile.

The tide had fallen. By the looks of things, it might even be reaching slack. He drifted toward the channel leading out of the bay. Black boulders that had been under water now cut the surface—or worse, lurked just beneath. The channel frothed as the tide raced out to sea, drawing the skiff with it. George had been floating without power; now he needed the motor, and fast, to make his ferry. Damn. It usually took between one and five pulls to start it, and in the way of many mechanical things, it tended to balk if he panicked.

He pulled the start-cord. Nothing. A second pull. Nothing. A third pull, and the Suzuki coughed to life. With his heart jumping, George wheeled back up the channel at full throttle, speeding away from the rocks he had been approaching too fast. The engine whined and buzzed, too full of air for his comfort—bad time to cavitate. He checked over his shoulder. Good, he had distanced himself from the worst of the boulders.

Back up in the bay, he reassessed. He thought of Brad and remembered his lifejacket. He pulled it out of the water on the floor, snapped the damp thing on, drifted, and felt the tidal current grab him again. It was fast, too fast. How could he trust the dinky motor to help him thread the rocks? His heart pounded as he tried to think.

The oars. He would row his way through.

Fitting the eight-foot oars into locks cost him time, but George got them in place and rowed. Too late, he thought, as the skiff crunched onto an underwater reef—a coward, his father used to call such below-surface sleepers. George felt the boat pivot on the rock mass, out of control. He shifted his weight, hoping the floor would slip free. It didn't work, didn't work—then it did. It was a bad scrape but hadn't ripped aluminum. Good.

He recovered and stroked hard as the boat swept toward a small comb of black boulders at the channel's edge. Cursing, he crabbed a blade that canted the boat, then saw the right gunnel tip so low it almost scooped water. Leaning left, he freed the diving oar from below surface. The boat righted.

His breath, full of fear now, sounded like a gale to him. If he fell out or capsized, the ice water would allow just fifteen minutes before numbing him senseless. That wouldn't be enough time for George to get to shore or anywhere; he had dropped out of swimming lessons before learning anything but dog-paddle. And there would be no rescue, no warm hold of a boat's cabin. No one would be there to save him. Everyone would be at the town square, laying out guideline ropes for the pole raising.

His mind leapt to terrible visions. He saw his lungs about to burst as he sunk and held his breath. He saw a first, tiny bubble leaving his lips, followed by an uncontrollable balloon of his last, precious oxygen, as his limbs turned to ice blocks.

Stop, George, stop, this doesn't help, he told himself. Ahead, the current foamed among rocks that had troubled him earlier. Now they stood higher, a stony arm a foot above water, reaching halfway across the channel. He would have to pull hard left to avoid a collision. Angling the boat to ferry, he felt water speed under the floor, hoping the leaking rivets wouldn't choose this moment to pop. The rock, wet and glinting with reflected light, lay in current that drew the skiff as if in command of its tiller. George needed more strength. He needed more power.

Time grew elastic. Seconds drew into long minutes that stretched and bent and filled with uncertainty. In those moments, George thought of his father's icy blackness. He saw his brothers' faces, now covered with ocean water and long sleep.

From memory, from somewhere, came the prayer: "Everlasting one! Everlasting one! Put your hand under us." Nothing. "Everlasting one! Everlasting one! Raise us up!"

Something shifted, something slight, some kind of lightening. He felt it and rowed so hard his oars bowed. He didn't watch his progress, just prayed and pulled. He rowed as hard as he thought it possible to row, pulled and groaned and didn't stop—then felt the current slow.

He stopped. If he pulled again, he'd shoot into shore. He had gotten left! He had done it! Breath darting like salmon avoiding a lure, he floated toward the smooth, open water of the inlet. Crumpled over the oars, he inhaled. With each breath his fear subsided. A trembling that had gripped him eased and ceased. As it did, his wonder grew at the prayer that had come from an unremembered place—something from Calvin? He didn't know. But where else?

"Thank you!" he called to the sky. Above him an eagle winged north toward town. At the top of his lungs, George called to it. "Thank you!"

He lifted his oars from the locks and set them back inside the boat. He moved to the rear of the skiff. With a single, purposeful tug, he pulled the cord, bringing the motor to life.

Aiming for town, he knew lights would be coming on in the square. Soon everyone would be invited to lift the pole. They would be rushing out of the darkness to help. He would see his mother there, and Calvin. The carver might not notice the skiff humming back across the inlet—he'd be too busy coordinating the crowd, making sure everyone got a chance to pull on the ropes. But he would see George join the crowd and would get him pulling, too.

George's sisters would nod their approval, in the warm breeze of the evening, at the fine string of pinks George would share with folks he had known since he was little—teachers from his grade school, friends who hadn't left for the big cities, the ones like him who didn't want to leave the waters they'd grown up on, no matter what costs they exacted. Those same waters gave a lot, too. They fed the world. They had brought the warden Brad to town, and his partner R.J., who would be there tonight, not asking any questions of George. Any newcomers could get their answers directly from Calvin and the native elders who would head the family tables as everyone sat down for the feast.

Acknowledgments

My deepest respect and admiration go to my maternal grandfather, Austin Frost of Nunda, New York. His manuscript, "Accelerating Theory of Earth Development: An Exposition" (1977), and his life as a naturalist, boatman, and amateur scientist inspired the story, "An Exposition of the Development of the Earth." Although he and I never achieved our dream of being coauthors, my grandfather's curiosity and passion for the outdoors live in me every day. My maternal grandmother, Marjorie Conrad Frost, lives on in my heart, too. She handed down a legacy of music, creativity, empathy, and support for the work of others.

My paternal grandfather, Russell Lawton, Sr., of Fall River, Massachusetts, died when I was very young. Images of him were captured in faded family photographs and movies on 8-mm film. They are all I recall of him. Throughout those movies, his gentle nature shines. My parents told me how much he had wanted to see his four grandchildren grown, to learn what we would make of our lives. Instead, a blood disease, possibly related to his work as a machinist, claimed him before I and my siblings grew out of grade school. My paternal grandmother, Jenny Cook Lawton, outlived him by three decades. An independent spirit and accomplished painter, she had an artist's eye that saw all.

These earlier Lawtons and Frosts inspired my love of nature, moving water, and artistic expression. More than that, they created family and community. Without them, these stories would not exist, nor would they have their roots in the natural world.

Deepest gratitude to my writing friends Lillian Howan, Jill Koenigsdorf, Karen Laws, and Z Egloff, who read and commented on early drafts of these stories. Much love to my husband Paul Christopulos and my daughter, Rose McMackin, who shared the journey to this modest book step-by-step. Many thanks, too, to all who supported the first publication of this work in 2014—what a huge act of faith it was for you all to dig into your own hard-earned funds when you hadn't even seen the first of these stories. Huge love and thanks to Kathryn Wilder, who first published the title story of this 2022 second edition and helped sponsor it in 2014.

Finally, my appreciation and thanks to Roger Real Drouin and all the staff at Little Curlew Press for adopting and publishing this collection in its original version, as *Steelies and Other Endangered Species: Stories on Water*. Little Curlew Press believes in the importance of wild places and free-flowing rivers. May their faith in these words and the critical nature of story shine in this new edition.

About the Author

Rebecca Lawton is an American author, fluvial geologist, and former Grand Canyon river guide. Her creative writing honors include a Fulbright Visiting Research Chair, Nautilus Book Award, Ellen Meloy Fund Award for Desert Writers, Pushcart Prize nominations, and residencies at Hedgebrook Retreat for Women Writers and The Island Institute. Visit her at beccalawton.com.

Also by Rebecca Lawton

Swimming Grand Canyon and Other Poems
(2021, Finishing Line Press)

The Oasis This Time:
Living and Dying with Water in the West
(2019, Torrey House Press)

Cool Writing Tips: A Month of What You'd Call Guidelines
(2016, Wavegirl Books)

Write Free: Attracting the Creative Life
(with Jordan Rosenfeld, 2016, Write Free Books)

Sacrament: Homage to a River
(with Geoff Fricker, 2013, Heyday)

Junction, Utah
(2013, van Haitsma Literary)

On Foot in Sonoma: Twelve Walks in the Valley of the Moon
(with Arthur Dawson, 2004, Kulupi Press)

Reading Water: Lessons from the River
(2002, Capital Books)

Discover Nature in the Rocks:
Things to Know and Things to Do
(with Diana Lawton, Susan Panttaja,
and Irene Guidici Ehret, 1997, Stackpole Books)

CPSIA information can be obtained
at www.ICGtesting.com
Printed in the USA
JSHW012301170323
39083JS00003B/19